Ho, Ho, Hey! What Just Happened?

Ho, Ho, Hey! What Just Happened?

Loretta Sinclair ©2010, 2014
Sinclair Publishing
P.O. Box 2052
Rancho Cordova, CA 95741-2052

Written by: Loretta Sinclair
Illustrated by: Melissa Perez

Ho, Ho, Hey! What Just Happened?

Title Page: *Ho, Ho, Hey! What Just Happened?*
Holiday enlightenment from an overworked Santa and his testy crew.

© 2010, 2014 by Loretta Sinclair. All rights reserved.
Sinclair Publishing, P.O. Box 2052, Rancho Cordova, CA 95741
www.sinclairinkspot.com; lori@sinclairinkspot.com
The ultimate design, content, editorial accuracy, and views expressed or implied in this work are solely those of the author.

Illustrated by Melissa Perez. ©2010, 2014
Selected artwork is the sole property of Melissa Perez, used here by permission. All Rights Reserved.

ISBN 13: 978-0-615-40432-5   ISBN 10: 0-615-40432-5
Library of Congress Catalog Card Number: 2010914063

Certain product brand names and organizations
are cited by name within this text.
Cited under United States copyright law, Chapter I, Section 107; Fair Use Limitations on Exclusive Rights, All Rights Reserved

All characters and entities, unless otherwise cited under applicable United States copyright law, appearing in this work are fictitious. Any resemblance to real persons, either living or dead, is purely coincidental. We all know the real Santa is a kind and loving individual who delights in giving gifts to children all over the world.

Merry Christmas to all!
~Lori

Ho, Ho, Hey! What Just Happened?

For my children, Chris and Kelly.
You are my strength and my inspiration.
Without you, nothing matters.

For the one true reason why we celebrate
Christmas every year. For the lover of my soul.
For the one man who gave up everything,
even unto life itself, so that I could live,
and live abundantly.

Happy Birthday, Jesus.

Ho, Ho, Hey! What Just Happened?

Ho, Ho, Hey! What Just Happened?

Table of Contents:

Ho, Ho, Hey! What Just Happened?

Blog, Humbug!

Christmas, Inc.
http://www.sinclairinkspot.com/the-impossibilities-blog

Hey all, Santa here. Listen, we've decided to start posting our progress for each Christmas season here on this blog. Hopefully, that will lessen the impact on our snail mail coming in, and free up some of Mrs. Clause's valuable time for other things. That's what she told me to say. I didn't actually know what a blog was until she made me sit down and listen. Here's how it works. In each entry we will try to address some past and current concerns, as well as keep everyone up to date on how we are doing. I'm still not sure how this whole thing is going to come together. We (Martha) hired a consulting firm to help with morale and negative public image. They all felt that we needed a little technology update. "Blast yourself into the 90's" I believe is how he put it. I'm still unclear on exactly how the internet, blog subscriptions, Twitter™, and Blackberry™ applications all work (I think I got all the words right there), but I gather that if I just type, then hit POST, you all can somehow magically see it. Don't bother writing in to explain it to me. I won't read it anyway. Just visit *http://www.sinclairinkspot.com/the-impossibilities-blog* for all your questions instead of writing to me and I'll be

Ho, Ho, Hey! What Just Happened?

happy. Right now I actually have work to do, so here's our guest blogger for this week: my beautiful wife, Martha Clause. Take it away, boss lady.

December 1

Hi all. I am so excited about Christmas this year. I thought in this first blog post I would give you all my secret recipe for Santa's favorite cookies: Oatmeal and Prune! He loves them, and can't get enough. I want everyone to make them, and leave him plenty this year. You know he eats everything that you leave out for him because he loves you all so much. He just can't get enough of these tasty morsels!

Of course the original recipe calls for raisins, but I replaced them with prunes so he won't get all "plugged up", as it were. You know when you get to be our age, your digestive tract needs just a little extra help. Also the oatmeal is a significant source of fiber, which aids in digestion and lowers cholesterol too. I also leave out the sugar. Can't have my Santa putting on too much weight. I know you all are used to a rolly, polly Santa but I need to keep his weight down. We all need to get used to the new slimmer, trimmer model. And speaking of fat, there is none in these cookies either. They scream health food all the way. Last year I put a huge batch of them in the sleigh before Santa left so he wouldn't run out of snacks on the road. The bag came back empty. That's proof enough for me how much he loves them!

So here it is, my secret recipe. And don't forget the egg nog!

Oatmeal Prune Cookies

Ingredients:

Ho, Ho, Hey! What Just Happened?

4 C instant cook oatmeal
1 bag large prunes
water to bind (you can use a little flavoring if you
like but I try not to spoil him too much)
2 large eggs to hold it all together

Combine all ingredients except the prunes into a bowl and stir until well mixed. You don't need any flour, we are on a gluten free kick these days. Leavening isn't necessary either since there is nothing that will rise. The dough may seem a little pasty and heavy but just keep stirring. (Don't use a wooden spoon, they tend to snap right about now.) That's the way it should be. Leave plenty of time to wash your hands, this stuff is a little sticky. Scoop onto cookie sheets and push 3 large prunes down into each cookie. They must be securely anchored to each one, not just sitting on top. Bake in a 500 degree oven for about 3-4 hours, or until dark and extra crispy. Sprinkle a little cinnamon over the top for an extra treat and to cover up some of the darkest brown coloring. No need to refrigerate or cover up. They stay hard and crunchy without any preservatives at all.

Enjoy~
Martha

Comment Santa: Oh good going Martha. Now I'm either going to be clogged up so bad a plunger won't help me, or a faucet that won't shut off. There's no way to tell which. Could go either way.

Comment Prancer: He tried to feed them to us last year. I broke my tooth and had to make an emergency landing at a dentist. Do you know how hard it is to find a veterinary dentist on Christmas Eve?

Comment Santa: About as hard as those cookies are! Ha! Last year we used some of them to fend off seagulls off the coast of California. I think we killed a few. Are they endangered?

Comment Vixen: Health food isn't all they scream! Can we pack some Pepto™ this year?

Comment Ivan, chief elf: Keep them coming folks. We don't have to mine for as much coal when we get these. Saves the elves from getting Black Lung Disease, and the naughty folks never know the difference.

Comment Martha: I don't know why I even try anymore.

Comment Prancer: Does that mean no cookies this year? Please?

◊

December 4

It's me, Santa.

Well here it is, that magical time of year. And once again I have to ask the question, have you all been good this year?

Ah, who are we kidding? I don't have to ask that question. I know what you've all been doing, and that most of you have been lying to cover it up! Shame on all of you!

I'm just doing this because my PR manager, (in cahoots with my wife) told me that I have to. So, I am going to pretend to be all cheery and wish everyone a

Ho, Ho, Hey! What Just Happened?

Merry Doggone Christmas when the truth is I wish I was doing something else. Nobody appreciates me. Nobody cares. Has any one of you ever written me a thank you card, ever? No. Not one. No manners at all, none of ya.

I work my butt off (wish it were actually true) making presents all year for people who don't appreciate it, don't want it, and either break it, or return in within a few days after Christmas. And don't bother posting any snide comments either. I'll just delete them all.

Merry Christmas!
Santa

Comment: Deleted by user
Comment: Deleted by user
Comment: Deleted by user

December 7

Hi all, Ivan here, otherwise known as the lead elf. I guess it's my turn to do this. I'm not really sure why I have to. Lord knows I have more important things to do, especially right now. But the big P.R. guy we hired said we needed to improve our public image. Personally I'd like to save the dough we're paying him and improve my wallet instead. And, I'm not the only one here that feels that way. We haven't had a raise in years. But, he said we had to do this, so here goes.

First I'd like to apologize again for the recall last year. When we contracted out all of our bicycle parts, we thought going overseas for the cheaper labor pool was in the best interests of everyone involved. We had no idea that the reason the bid was so much less than everyone else was because they left out every other wheel spoke on the bikes. Do you know how many bikes we deliver every year? We're talking hundreds of thousands of spokes. Cheapskates. The least they could have done was tell us. Anyway, we're all very glad little Johnny recovered so quickly and there were no more claims against our liability insurance. That should help keep costs down this year. You will all be glad to know that we have brought all of our labor contracts back home this year so the elves are busy once again making all of your crap.

Also, the salmonella thing. Sorry about that too. When it was pitched to us to deliver eggs decorated like Christmas rather than Easter, we thought it was a great idea. The first shipments arrived in late August, but the boxes were not marked "Keep Refrigerated." We had no idea that they were real eggs, and were perishable. I understand that some of you were lucky. The dogs in your households took the eggs and buried them in the back yard. Kudos to all the pooches that saved the day. Warehousing has been made aware in their contract matrix that all shipments from this manufacturer are to be refrigerated until delivery. We will also be delivering complimentary Imodium™ this year in case there are any other errant snacking issues. We got a big advertizing bonus from them over it. Opportunists. So you can all quit sending me hate mail. I don't really care what you think anyway, including your parents. The only reason I apologized was because the lawyers made us do it to avoid litigation. And just for the record, I think you all suck too. As far as what we have in store for this year, well, that's still a secret. We can't ruin the surprise. You'll just have to wait 18 more days like the rest of us. Hey, I have an idea. In order to help pass the time, why don't you all GET A JOB AND QUIT BOTHERING ME! Merry Christmas.

Ivan

Ho, Ho, Hey! What Just Happened?

Comment PR Consulting: I told you to let me review your blog before you posted it.

Comment Ivan: Bite me.

Comment PR Consulting > Santa: Santa, we need an urgent meeting.

Comment Santa: Why do I have to be involved in this? I didn't say it.

Comment PR Consulting>Santa: You're in charge. You're also supposed to be posting a blog every day.

Comment Santa: Who has time? I can't even find time for a meeting with you over all this garbage.

Comment Martha: I'll be there.

Comment Rudolph: Uh Oh. That's gonna hurt.

December 9

Take it away reindeer.

Ok, first of all we don't like being called reindeer anymore. It has a negative connotation. You humans all think of reindeer as pack animals, beasts of burden. Stupid creatures that do nothing but walk, eat, breed, and occasionally sleep. We are so much more than that. We have a very important job. Without us, Christmas would never happen. Nothing would be delivered. Nothing. We are now demanding the respect that we deserve and have not gotten for years. On top of the fact that we are

Ho, Ho, Hey! What Just Happened?

not just ordinary reindeer, but reindeer that can fly. You show me anywhere else in the world where any distant relative of ours can do that. Ha! You can't! Because they can't. So from now on, instead of being called Santa's reindeer (he doesn't own us, by the way, despite public perception) we are calling ourselves the North Pole Nine. So here we go on this blog thing that we've been told have to do for morale. (Whose morale, I'm not sure.) Each of us nine will make a brief statement, and then get back to our reindeer games before halftime. I'll finish off at the end. Let's take it in order.

Rudolph.

Dasher:

I don't know why Rudolph thinks he's in charge all the time, telling us what to do. Strap a flashlight on his head and all the sudden he has to run everything.

Dancer:

We've petitioned the union to change the order of the reindeer on the sleigh from year to year. We're going to go to a seniority based system to be more fair. It's all subject to the union vote, and negotiations with management. Don't know exactly what that will do to all your cutsie little Christmas songs, but you'll just have to deal with that. I want a turn to lead the sleigh too.

Prancer:

Everyone must try and stay in step this year so we don't look like a bunch of dance class trainees again. We all need to take the same steps, at the same time so we look like a well oiled machine. We should all be going the same speed, the same direction, at the same time. No one should be flying off ahead just to prove that they are faster. Got it?

Ho, Ho, Hey! What Just Happened?

Vixen:

It's a dream come true for a girl flying in this squad with all these big hunky men. There are just so many to choose from. What's a girl to do?

Comet:

Full speed ahead! Everyone out of my way.

Cupid:

I think Vixen would make a great couple with Blitzen. Their names would be too hard to say together though. "We're having Vixen and Blitzen over." Too confusing. Besides, Blitzen is already in a registered domestic partnership with Anastasia from across the Bering Sea. I think Donner likes her though - Vixen that is. What do you all think?

Donner:

It's really hard to fly with her cute little behind wagging in front of me like that.

Blitzen:

So they put the old man of the crew in the back again. That's okay. I've put in my time. I'm just waiting for my retirement papers to be approved so I can be put out to pasture. Let the young ones pull their weight. I've done my time.

Rudolph;

So there you have it. All the news from the North Pole Nine. Take care everyone, and we'll see you all on Christmas Eve.

Comment PR Consulting > Santa: You didn't tell me you had union troubles.

Comment User Post<Johnny's parents: Hey Santa, bring

Ho, Ho, Hey! What Just Happened?

your pooper scooper this year. I'm getting tired of the packages left out front for me.

Comment Santa: I don't own them. They're not my pets. Check your county ordinances regarding fouling from strays. Not my problem.

◊

December 13

Santa, I believe it's your turn again, darling. Love, Martha

Comment Santa>Martha: Martha, if you loved me, you'd help me out a little more, and don't call me darling in front of the elves. You know I hate that.

Comment Martha>Santa: Yea, well if you loved me you'd find some time to spend with me instead of always playing with those little green pains.

Comment Ivan>Martha: Who you calling a pain? We were doing just fine until you started getting all bossy!

Comment PR Consulting>Everyone: Knock it off! Meeting. NOW!

Comment Santa>Martha: Great, see what you started!

◊

December 17

Hi all. It's Martha Clause again, back with some more great Christmas cheer. It won't be long now. Only 8 more days. I know you're all excited, so I

Ho, Ho, Hey! What Just Happened?

thought I'd share another one of Santa's favorite recipes. This is another special request that I get every year. I know there will be lots of comments at the end of this post so make time to read them all.

Aside from having an obvious weight problem, high blood pressure, and cholesterol problems, my poor Santa also suffers from diverticulitis. For those of you who don't know what that is, it means inflammation of the colon. And let me tell you, when he gets it, he can be a real pain in the arse. He gets bloated, abdominal pains, horrible gas. I mean not just regular gas either, as if that isn't bad enough. He gets farts that smell like something crawled up there and died. Ohhh! I tell ya, that'll ruin the appetite of everyone in the house. We all lose weight when Santa has a flare up. So here's what I do to keep him in check.

Stress is one of the biggest causes for flare ups. Unfortunately there isn't really anything that I can do about that, at least not at this time of year. The schedule is tight and I can't help that. I just have to do the best I can. I prepare healthy well-balanced meals and make sure he has them to go. No more fast food. High fat is bad. Breakfast consists of waffles and sugar free syrup. I use a little bit of butter, just for flavor and to keep my man happy. Two waffles, with a piece of fruit on the side usually does it, along with a big glass of milk.

Lunch is a sandwich on whole wheat toast and some sort of lunch meat. My Santa likes cheese, so I use the low fat kind. There are some baked chips to go along with it, a cup of hot coffee, and a couple of the Prune Oatmeal cookies that I posted earlier.

Snack in the afternoon is some carrots and a soda (Santa likes anything with bubbles; a trait that has gotten him in trouble on more than one occasion).

Dinner always starts with a glass of red wine, or two, or three... We have some grilled fish - usually salmon. We grill it outside due to the smell. Lots of butter and lemon on top. Brussel sprouts for the side, and mashed peanut butter potatoes with chocolate chips on top. Sounds disgusting, but he loves it. Dessert is a must. We try to keep it healthy and delicious. Ice cream and onions, with mustard on top. It's a recipe that has been handed down through the generations, a personal favorite of my grandfather's. It takes a little getting used to, but once you've acquired the taste, it'll stay with you forever, along with a little gas.

Now here's the secret. Two words: baby food. He can't have anything that is going to get stuck in the little nooks and crannies of his insides (I saw a picture at the doctor's office, kinda gross). So, if we grind it up, puree, frappe, chop, mince, prepare, process, and pre-digest, then he doesn't have a problem. It's easy. A general rule of thumb, if he doesn't have to chew, then he doesn't have gas. This, of course, is just what we do here in this house. For your arse-pains, things might be a little different. I think you're all going to like this, though. Prepare all meals as listed above, at the same time. Take them all, throw everything into an industrial size food processor or blender, add enough liquid (your choice, of course, you can use water, milk, or vodka) to make into a thick, smoothie consistency, and put into travel safe containers. Then, he can have all three meals, plus snack and dessert every time he takes a swig. It's perfect. Complete nutrition on the go. What could be healthier or more convenient than that? I'm thinking about marketing it. It'll sell big I'm sure.

So there you go. I'm setting the whole afternoon aside to answer all of your questions and posts. Can't wait to hear from you all. Please consider making something like this to leave for Santa on Christmas Eve this year. I know he'll appreciate all your

thoughtfulness.
   Martha.

Comment Martha: Questions? Anyone?

December 20

   Now for all the news from the elves, take it away Ivan.

Comment Ivan: I'm busy.

Comment PR Consulting>Ivan: We're all working together on this, remember?

Comment Ivan>PR Consulting: Bite me.

◊

December 23

   I don't know what to say anymore. I give up.
Santa

Comment PR Consulting>Santa: I quit. You'll get my bill.

Visit *http://www.sinclairinkspot.com/the-impossibilities-blog*
for more musings from your favorite Christmas characters.

Ho, Ho, Hey! What Just Happened?

Can You Hear Me Now?

"Customer service. This is Mary P. What is your phone number please?"

"1-800-TOY-DUDE"

"How may I help you, sir?"

"I have been on hold for over an hour," the angry man snapped. "What kind of operation are you people running over there?"

"I'm sorry for the delay sir, but it *is* Christmas Eve. This is our busiest time of the year."

"Mine too!" the man screamed into the phone. "And I don't have time for games. This is an emergency."

"Well I'll certainly do the best I can for you, sir. What is your emergency?"

"I've lost my phone and I need it back," he said.

"We can get you a new phone right away," Mary P. answered. "I can get one there overnight for an additional charge."

"I don't need a new phone, I need MY phone. It has some important stuff on it."

"I'm sure it does, let me just check your account. Last name please."

"Kringle."

"Spell that please."

Ho, Ho, Hey! What Just Happened?

"K-R-I-N-G-L-E"

"First name?"

"Kris."

"Checking, can I place you on hold please?"

"No, I don't have time to - - -"

Click.

"Hello. Hellooo!" Santa slammed his fist on the table. "MARTHA!"

"Don't you yell at me," Martha snapped. "I told you, you lost the phone, you replace it."

"I can't replace it. I need the phone that YOU put the Naughty and Nice list on. You're the one that wanted to upgrade."

"You still used pencil and paper."

"You mean cordless laptop with wireless remote?" Santa snapped.

"Sarcasm won't help right now," Martha shot back.

"Sir," the voice on the phone interrupted. "I don't seem to have a Christopher Kringle."

"That's because I didn't say Christopher, I said Kris, with K."

"Checking."

"And don't put me on- - -"

Click.

"- - - hold! Martha!"

"I told you not to take the phone outside."

"I had to go outside. The phone YOU got me doesn't get any reception in the house!"

"Then you should have brought the phone back in with you when you came in, and don't yell at me like that." She smirked.

"Martha, please, it's been Christmas Eve for three days now and I haven't even left yet."

"I've found it sir," Mary P. said. "What can I do for you?"

Ho, Ho, Hey! What Just Happened?

"I've lost my phone," Santa said again, "and I need it back."

"Yes sir, what kind of phone did you have?"

"Red."

"I'm sorry sir?"

"Red. It's a red phone."

"What is the brand name and model?"

"I don't know. You see I didn't buy it. My wife gave it to me and SHE WON"T HELP ME RIGHT NOW BECAUSE SHE'S MAD!"

"I see. So you don't have any idea what kind of phone you had?"

"I think the box said it was a Blackbird."

"A Blackbird? Sir, there's no such thing."

"I don't know. Don't you people have records for that?"

"Yes, we do, but I need to confirm your identity before I can continue, so I need to know what kind of equipment you have in order to proceed. It's a confidentiality issue."

"Look, Mary P., I don't know what it was called. It was a gift. My LOVING WIFE got it for me and she put some extremely valuable information on there. And I SCREWED UP and LOST IT, so now I need it back AND SHE WON'T HELP ME! I'm sorry that I can't tell you the serial number and the size and color of the box that it came in."

"Can you describe the phone please," Mary asked.

"Look," Santa said, trying to keep calm, "it had a big screen, and little pictures on there. I touched the picture that looks like a piece of paper, and my list came up. It is a very *important* list at this time of year. It tells me my delivery schedules, and type of gifts that people are to receive. Do you understand now?"

"Yes sir", Mary P. continued. "For confirmation purposes, did you have any other equipment?"

Ho, Ho, Hey! What Just Happened?

Santa sighed. This would not be easy. He settled in for a long winter's phone call.

"I had some kind of hands free thing for my slei- --, uh, my vehicle. It's the law now."

"And do you know the brand name and model of that?"

"Blue something. You push the little button first, then dial. It was called a, uh- - -. Oh, reindeer snot! I can't remember."

"Did you just swear?" Martha jumped in.

"Santa doesn't swear, Martha!" he shot back.

"Santa? I thought you said your name was Kris Kringle. Sir, who am I speaking to?" Mary P. demanded.

"I *am* Kris Kringle. My wife just likes to call me names."

"I'm sure," Mary P. sighed. "Please continue with your equipment."

"Blue dentures... Blue bird... Blue fruit. Blueberry... Blueberry! That's what I have. My phone was a Blueberry touch screen phone with a hands free BlueBird denture thing. I need it back."

"Sir, I think you mean a Blackberry™ with a Blue Tooth™ set."

"Nope. It's not. It's a Blueberry." He turned to the doorway. "So there Martha! I remembered without you! Ha!" he said into the phone. "She didn't think I could do it. She thinks she knows everything!"

Mary P. sighed. "Ok, Mr. Kringle. Let's proceed."

"Yes, let's. I'm in rather a hurry as you can imagine."

"Uh oh," she said, "hmmm."

"What?" Santa asked.

"You don't seem to have any insurance on your phone."

"What does that mean?"

Ho, Ho, Hey! What Just Happened?

"With insurance on your phone, it is replaced at no cost to you if it is lost or stolen. You also don't seem to be eligible for an upgrade at this time either. You have to be 75% of the way through your contract for that."

"What contract?"

"Sir, when you signed up for wireless service with us you signed a contract. You can get a new phone every two years, but must be a minimum of 75% through your two year contract period before I can do that."

"But I don't want a new phone, I want MY phone."

"Unfortunately sir, since YOU lost it, I can't exactly fly out there and find it for you now can I?"

"That's a little snotty Mary P. Tell me what does the P stand for?"

"I'm not going to tell you."

"Well then, let me guess. Is it Pritchard? or Pleasant? - no that can't be right. Or maybe it is Mary Pain-in-the-arse, because that's what you're being right now."

"Stop swearing!" Martha screamed.

"I'm not swearing!" Santa yelled back.

"If I had my list right now Mary P. I'd- - - "

"You'd what?" Mary snapped back, her tone noticeably hostile. "Well you don't, now do you?" she said. "So now you have to start your list all over again. Which means that everyone starts out on the nice side, and when they screw up, they get moved over. As long as you don't know who I am, you can't do that. So there, Santa. Take that."

Santa was stunned.

"You sit up there all high and mighty on your North Pole throne passing judgment on the rest of us. How dare you? You don't know what it's like to have a real job. You don't have real problems like the rest of us do. Life's all fun and reindeer games for you isn't it?"

"I don't judge people."

Ho, Ho, Hey! What Just Happened?

"Oh yes you do. You alone decide what they get and don't get for Christmas every year. Perhaps you could explain why I *never* seem to get anything that I ever ask for."

Santa was speechless. He decided to try a different tactic.

"Look, Mary. I'm just trying to do my job here, and it gets a little stressful this time of year as you can imagine. Perhaps I overlooked a thing or two in the past."

"Job? Are you kidding me? That's not a real job. One day a year you get in your car and deliver a few toys. Try getting up day after day, year after year, listening to people complain that they lost their phones so you somehow are obligated to make it right. Everything is somehow my fault, and I get yelled at for their stupidity. And for what? To have my self-esteem bashed by every single caller who thinks that they are more important than I am, and a lousy paycheck that will barely cover my rent? Don't you dare sit here and tell me you have a stressful job."

"So you're not going to help me at all, are you?" he asked.

"Ok, listen up, fat man," she said. NO PHONE!"

"No phone! Just like that? Blazing Jupiter woman! Whatever happened to customer service?"

"I told you not to swear at her," Martha jumped in.

"I didn't swear!" Santa shot back. "I swear..." he muttered.

"I heard that!" Martha yelled over her shoulder as she ran through the door behind Santa and out to the packed sleigh parked just outside.

"So did I," Mary P. said. "So on top everything else, you're a liar now too."

"I didn't lie. What are you talking about?" he said back into the phone.

Ho, Ho, Hey! What Just Happened?

"What am I talking about? You just said- - - "

Crash!

"Mary, I'm sorry but I have to place you on hold for a minute." Santa laid the phone down amid an angry verbal onslaught and turned to the banging and crashing through the open door behind him.

"Martha, what on earth are you doing?"

"Little Johnnie L. asked for either a new phone or a sled. We gave him a phone. I'll have the elves throw in a sled and you can take his phone instead. He'll never know the difference"

"That's all well and good, but I there is still the matter of the lost list. I can't deliver anything without it. What are we going to do about that?"

"We?" Martha asked.

"Please, Martha, I'm begging you. I'll take you on that vacation you've been nagging me about as soon as I get back. I promise. Just help me get through - - - "

"It's on the memory card."

"What card?"

"I saved the list on a memory card. I pulled it out to update it right before you lost your phone. All we have to do is activate the new phone and plug the card in. You'll be back in business in a few minutes."

"Do you think maybe you could have told me this before now?"

"I forgot."

Santa glared at his wife. "You forgot? It's a *memory* card."

"Hey, it's not easy being Mrs. Clause. You try being in charge of You. See what that feels like."

"Ok. Ok. So, we're good to go now, right."

"Just as soon as you get that helpful little honey on the phone to activate this phone," she said, handing him a neatly wrapped package.

"Do you want me to do it?"

Ho, Ho, Hey! What Just Happened?

"No, no," Santa smiled, for the first time today. "I can take care of that." He ran back to the phone.

"Mary P!" he said in his booming jovial voice, "Santa here. Listen, turns out Martha had the Naughty and Nice list saved on a memory card the whole time, and we have located a new BlueBird phone that we just need activated, then I am back in business. So, with your assistance please, I'd like to get back to work. This call's being recorded for training purposes, right?"

"Uhhh, of course, s-s-sir," she stuttered. "I would be happy to ass-ss-ss-ist you. Let me just check your r-r-records one more t-t-time."

"Of course," Santa boomed. "And while we're at it, I'll need a little information from you too. Let's start with full name, address, brothers and sisters, and, parents. Oh, and just for laughs, what is *your* phone number please?"

Ho, Ho, Hey! What Just Happened?

Ho, Ho, H.O.A.

North Pole Home Owner's Association
P.O. Box 0
North Pole, Arctic Ocean
...Where the magic of Christmas lives every day

Dear Mr. Kringle:

A complaint has been filed by some of your neighbors who wish to remain anonymous at this time regarding barking dogs at your residence. This noise is extremely distressing to them and they wish to make it stop. Perhaps you are not aware, but the Homeowner's Association has a clause in the CC&R's (Codes, Covenants, and Restrictions) that you signed when you purchased said residence. It clearly states:

All household pets, including but not limited to, dogs, cats, birds, and other small domesticated household animals, shall be under the control of the homeowner at all times. Said animals shall not be permitted to emit chronic noise making that would be disturbing to other residents. Such noise making is defined as barking, yarking, howling, growling, grunting, or any other utterance that could be distressing or disruptive to other households.

The noise that has been described as coming from your residence is that of a loud whistle. Not really a whistle though. More like a whistle crossed with a high pitched yowling. It's not exactly a howl, or a growl, per se. One resident said it sounded like a moose. Anyway, please make every effort to control your dogs so that your neighbors are not disturbed in the future.

Sincerely,

Miss Priss
North Pole HOA

◊

Kris Kringle
P.O. Box 00
North Pole, Frozen Mass in the Middle of the Arctic Ocean
Middle of Nowhere

Dear Miss Priss:

I have no dogs, and dogs don't whistle, nor do they yowl. Tell my neighbors to mind their own business.

Sincerely,

K. Kringle

◊

Dear Mr. Kringle:

I have received a clarification from your complainant neighbors. It is not dogs that have been witnessed on your property, but rather something akin to livestock. There appear to be nine large moose-like creatures, one with a bright red light source, that are roaming around your property. It is the snorting, stomping, and bleating from these creatures that is disruptive to your neighbors. Also, for our records, we are requiring proof of county licensing registration for said animals. Please send copies immediately.

You have fencing on your property. Please make sure that your fencing is made of approved materials, and is up to the standard of the Homeowner's Association requirements. In addition, the fencing must be able to contain your pets, and prevent them from wandering the neighborhood. Your animals have been witnessed leaping and bounding over your property lines and onto adjoining properties. There have been additional complaints of fecal matter being deposited in the neighborhood and it has been attributed to your household.

Please tend to your pets.

Sincerely,

Miss Priss

◊

Dear Miss Priss:

These animals are not my pets. Ask them. They belong to no one. Moreover, Caribou are not capable of leaping over fencing that is nearly eight feet high. Tell my neighbors to lay off the egg nog, and to quit peering into my windows with their binoculars. They can wait until Christmas morning just like everyone else.

Additionally, livestock, or other large creatures are not covered under the CC&R's that were signed by myself and my fellow residents. It covers *"all household pets, including but not limited to, dogs, cats, birds, and other small domesticated household* _animals._ " Clearly, Caribou are not small domesticated household pets, and can be considered nothing but wild animals (and if you knew them, you would know how wild they really are). I cannot be held accountable for them. If these wild animals choose to defecate outside my property, then the recipient homeowner is responsible for clean up. Please have them reference the county ordinance regarding fouling of private property by strays and wild animals. If they wish to continue to blame me for the fecal matter, then I must insist on a DNA test, and proof of ownership.

Please inform my neighbors that I am extremely busy right now, and do not have time for this garbage

Sincerely,

Kris Kringle

◊

Dear Mr. Kringle:

If they are not your pets, then why have you been seen feeding them?

Additionally, your last letter brings up yet another concern by your neighbors. They have been witness to you operating an unlicensed business from your home. Numerous delivery trucks have been seen coming and going from your residence, and a sizeable inventory can been seen in your garage area when the doors are left up. Please be aware that it is also a violation of the CC&R's to use your garage space for storage. It must be used for your vehicle only. Please clean out your garage immediately and send us a photograph for our records to show that the violation has been cleared. Additionally, please send copies of your business license and permits to operate a business in a private residence. We will also need a copy of your workers compensation insurance policy to cover the employees that you have. Your employees are also reportedly quite small. Are you aware of the child labor laws in this country? Please provide a listing of all staff including their ages, hours, salaries, and guardian information so that we may ensure that no laws are being broken.

Sincerely,

Miss Priss

◊

Dear Miss Priss

Yes, I feed the animals. In case you haven't noticed, our home sits on a floating mass of ice in the middle of the Arctic Ocean. Nothing grows here. If these animals were not fed they would starve. I am forwarding a copy of your demand letter to the headquarters of both P.E.T.A.® and Greenpeace®. I find your indifference to the lives of these gentle giants unconscionable. You can expect to hear from them regarding your instituted policy of cruelty to animals.

I do not operate a business of any kind from my home. Toy making is a hobby. I have no staff, nor do I collect any paychecks. My garage is filled with tools for my trade. If you require a picture of my garage for your records, then I suggest that you come and take it. Please make an appointment first, as I am extremely busy this time of year. I also do not have time for frivolous correspondence. I go through a mountain of important mail every day regarding my responsibilities and delivery schedule. Once again, tell my neighbors to mind their own business. You can also inform them that it is against the law to go through my trash receptacle at the end of my driveway. It is extremely low class to pull out broken and discarded items from someone else's trash to take home to your own family. Tell them to man-up and buy some toys for their kids instead of taking my throw-aways. It is also trespassing to come onto my property looking for leftover pieces, and to spy on my household. If they do not cease this action immediately, I will take legal action, as well as move them to the naughty list. They will know what this means.

Sincerely,

K. Kringle

◊

Dear Mr. Kringle:

Let me assure you that I have no policy of animal cruelty. If the creatures are indeed wild, and wish to graze on your property then they may certainly do so. The Homeowner's Association is happy to entertain the wild and natural habitat of the North Pole. We exist to protect the delicate nature and beauty of the pole. We wish only to preserve our way of life for future generations.

We still have some concerns regarding the Caribou, though. It seems as though you have named them, and there seems to be one that is a clear leader. They appear to be organized, and have been witnessed playing some sort of reindeer games, perhaps even to the level of an Olympics. This is not done in the wild, and leads to the theory that they have indeed been domesticated, and may, in fact, be pets. They have also been seen jumping to heights impossible for any animal of their size and stature to reach. It has been described as "flying." Do you have a response to this Mr. Kringle?

Sincerely,

Miss Priss

◊

Prissy:

Flying reindeer? Who do they think I am, Santa Clause?

Kris

◊

Kris:

Sir, there's no such thing as Santa. Don't be naive.

The neighbors' complaints are being dismissed as inconclusive. Please pardon the interruption to your busy schedule.

Sincerely,

Miss Priss

North Pole Homeowner's Association
...*Where the magic of Christmas lives every day.*

Ho, Ho, Hey! What Just Happened?

Home Tweet Home

"Ok, listen up," Martha yelled at the Christmas crew. "We have a new procedure this year."

"When is she going to stop changing things?"

Santa shrugged.

"You need to stop her." Ivan, Santa's elf foreman folded his arms across the front of his little green velvet suit and glared at his boss. "This is getting out of control."

"Shhh. You're going to get me in trouble."

"Oh, so that's how it is?" Ivan demanded.

"Hey, *you* try and live with her!" Santa said.

The room fell silent. All eyes turned forward.

"If you two are done, can I have your attention please." Martha was staring over her wire rimmed glasses at the two in the back of the room. "Are we ready now?"

"Yes ma'am," they both answered, looking down.

"All right then," she continued. "As I was saying, we have a new procedure this year. I am tired of having you guys leave for weeks at a time with no word on where you are, and what's going on. So, I have set up cell phones with internet access for each of you. I have also set everyone up with Twitter® accounts. Starting on Christmas Eve, you are all going to take your cell phones with you on your deliveries. I want you to post tweets of your progress and problems along that way. That way I know where everyone is, and what the status of Christmas is. It's a single night for the rest of the world, but for those of us involved in the whole 'time standing still' thing, it's the longest night of the year. Plus, I won't have to worry about anyone laying dead in a ditch anymore because I haven't heard from you in hours or days. Everyone understand?"

"Yes, ma'am," the whole room answered, afraid not to.

"Santa, you're first."

Santa stood and walked to the front of the room. He was handed a cell phone. "Your Twitter ID® is **@S_man_twit.**

"Oh, that's cool." Santa smiled. He turned and looked at his crew behind him. "I'm the S_man."

"You mean you're a twit!" Rudolph giggled. The elves all joined in.

"Rudy, you're next."

"Oh man! Why do I have to have one of those things?" Rudolph pouted.

"Get up here, Martha said. "You're **@I_can_fly_twit**".

"I can't carry that thing. I don't have any hands to type. Plus, I'll be flying. Do you want me to get into an accident? I'm pretty sure that's illegal."

"For you," Martha said, "I have a voice activated software. It will hang from a strap around your neck. All you have to do is to speak." Martha placed the leather lanyard around his neck. Rudy hung his head low and shook it, hoping the phone would fall off at some point, but it caught on his antler and just wiggled. He heard giggles from the back of the room.

"Looks like you're a twit too," Ivan laughed out loud.

"Ivan, you're **@Toys_r_4_twits.**"

"That's pretty accurate," he mused, "but why do I need one of those things? I don't leave the North Pole."

Ho, Ho, Hey! What Just Happened?

"This year, when one of the toys is damaged or lost I am going to have you fly out to Santa to replace it rather than using UPS® as we have done in the past. Our overnight bill is outrageous. You can take one of the reindeer trainees, but keep in touch while you're gone."

Ivan shook his head and gave Santa a sharp look.

"And I," Martha said smiling, "am **@Santas_twit**."

The whole room smiled at that.

"I have already set up apps on your phones, and everyone is already following everyone else in your Twitter® accounts. So, when you post your updates, everyone will be able to see what everyone else is doing. I can also keep tabs on all of you at one time, and make sure that things continue to flow smoothly. Any questions?"

The room was silent.

"Good," Martha said. "Off with you then."

◊

@Santas_twit: Good luck everyone. #merry
Martha: 11:59 PM Dec. 24 from web

@Santas_twit: What's the weather like out there?
Martha: 11:59 PM Dec. 24 from web

@Santas_twit: Have the first deliveries been made yet?
Martha: 11:59 PM Dec. 24 from web

@Santas_twit: Why am I the only one tweeting?
#answerme
Martha: 11:59 PM Dec. 24 from web

@Toys_r_4_twits: Why do all the tweets have the same time on them?
Ivan: 11:59 PM Dec. 24 from web

Ho, Ho, Hey! What Just Happened?

@Santas_twit: Because time stands still tonight. Geez,
Ivan. How long have you worked here
now? #duh
Martha: 11:59 PM Dec. 24 from web

@Toys_r_4_twits: Obviously too long. I don't know
why we have to this anyway. #stupid.
Ivan: 11:59 PM Dec. 24 from web

@Santas_twit: Because I said so. #boss
Martha: 11:59 PM Dec. 24 from web

@Santas_twit: Santa, you out there?
Martha: 11:59 PM Dec. 24 from web

@S_man_twit: I'm a little busy right now Martha.
Could you cut me some slack please.
Rudy's got us off track. Don't know
where I am. #busy
Santa: 11:59 PM Dec. 24 from txt

@I_can_fly_twit: I can barely see where I am going.
Nose is turned on high, but it's running
so everything is blurry.
Rudolph: 11:59 PM Dec. 24 from txt

@S_man_twit: I told you to blow it before we left the
house! #ewww #snot
Santa: 11:59 PM Dec. 24 from txt

@I_can_fly_twit: Where's your GPS? #biteme
Rudolph: 11:59 PM Dec. 24 from txt

@S_man_twit: Forgot it. You should know the route by
now. This isn't the first time we've been
out here. #duh
Santa: 11:59 PM Dec. 24 from txt

Ho, Ho, Hey! What Just Happened?

@Santas_twit: Ok, guys. It's gonna be a long month
tonight. #everybodycalmdown
Martha: 11:59 PM Dec. 24 from web

@S_man_twit: Ok, we made it to the first stop. Almost
skidded off the roof. May have damaged
the runners on the sleigh. Looks like
someone forgot to pack the chains again.
Santa: 11:59 PM Dec. 24 from txt

@Toys_r_4_twits: Why is everything always my fault?
Ivan: 11:59 PM Dec. 24 from web

@S_man_twit: Because you were supposed to pack
them. #stupid
Santa: 11:59 PM Dec. 24 from txt

@Toys_r_4_twits: So you can forget the GPS but I can't
forget the chains? #unfair
Ivan: 11:59 PM Dec. 24 from web

@S_man_twit: Life isn't fair. Roofs are icy and snow
everywhere. It's dangerous out here.
#getoverit
Santa: 11:59 PM Dec. 24 from txt

@Toys_r_4_twits: Well excuuuussse me! So I forgot to
pack them again. Crucify me why don't
ya? This new procedure sucks. All this
extra work is stupid. #onstrike
Ivan: 11:59 PM Dec. 24 from web

@Toys_r_4_twits: Seriously, Santa. I don't know why
you let her run your life like that. You
need to stop her before she ruins
Christmas! Who wears the pants around
here anyway? #marthabuttout
Ivan: 11:59 PM Dec. 24 from web

Ho, Ho, Hey! What Just Happened?

@Toys_r_4_twits: Wait. Can she read this? #uhoh
Ivan: 11:59 PM Dec. 24 from txt

@S_man_twit: Yes.
Santa: 11:59 PM Dec. 24 from web

@I_can_fly_twit: Nice going, runt. Now she's ticked.
Rudolph: 11:59 PM Dec. 24 from web

@S_man_twit: Martha? #ohcrap
Santa: 11:59 PM Dec. 24 from txt

@S_man_twit: Martha?
Santa: 11:59 PM Dec. 24 from txt

@Toys_r_4_twits: Um, Mrs. Clause is assisting me in
the workshop for a minute. Hold please.
Ivan: 11:59 PM Dec. 24 from web

@I_can_fly_twit: Bet he has trouble sitting down.
#butthurt
Rudolph: 11:59 PM Dec. 24 from txt

@S_man_twit: Wish I could see it. #hahaha
Santa: 11:59 PM Dec. 24 from txt

@I_can_fly_twit: Yeah, that's gonna leave a mark.
Rudolph: 11:59 PM Dec. 24 from txt

@S_man_twit: Let's keep moving. We have a lot of
ground to cover tonight. #getbacktowork
Santa: 11:59 PM Dec. 24 from txt

@I_can_fly_twit: Roger that. #fatman
Rudolph: 11:59 PM Dec. 24 from txt

@S_man_twit: And be careful where you step. You
almost broke that doll I dropped.
Santa: 11:59 PM Dec. 24 from txt

Ho, Ho, Hey! What Just Happened?

@I_can_fly_twit: Don't drop them and I won't step on
them, genius. #duh
Rudolph:11:59 PM Dec. 24 from txt

@I_can_fly_twit: Ouch! Watch those reins. That hurt.
Rudolph: 11:59 PM Dec. 24 from txt

@S_man_twit: Sorry, my bad. Just watch your feet...
All four of them. #hahaha
Santa: 11:59 PM Dec. 24 from txt

@Santas_twit: Let me know when you leave the
continent. I am keeping a spreadsheet of your progress.
That way I know where you are.
Martha: 11:59 PM Dec. 24 from web

@S_man_twit: Yes ma'am. #whipped
Santa: 11:59 PM Dec. 24 from txt

@S_man_twit: Okay, just left the Pacific coastline and
over the ocean now, heading toward
Hawaii. #flyinghigh
Santa: 11:59 PM Dec. 24 from txt

@Santas_twit: Got it. You didn't forget Canada again
did you? #dipstick
Martha: 11:59 PM Dec. 24 from web

@S_man_twit: Nope. Canada's good. Blitzen's looking
a little green though. Did you remember
his Dramamine™? #gonnapuke
Santa: 11:59 PM Dec. 24 from txt

@Santas_twit: #Uh Oh. I set it out. Let me check.
Martha: 11:59 PM Dec. 24 from web

Ho, Ho, Hey! What Just Happened?

@S_man_twit: Don't bother checking Martha. I can tell you - YOU FORGOT! He just puked and we flew right into it. #gagme
Santa: 11:59 PM Dec. 24 from txt

@I_can_fly_twit: Ewwwww!
Rudolph: 11:59 PM Dec. 24 from txt

@S_man_twit: Mayday, Mayday, Mayday. We need an emergency landing on the aircraft carrier USS Nimitz. Have experienced a toxic waste spill. Condition: Urgent. Please reply. #desperate
Santa: 11:59 PM Dec. 24 from txt

@Nimitz_twit: Roger that, Santa. You are cleared to land. #herewegoagain
USS Nimitz:11:59 PM Dec. 24 from radio

@S_man_twit: Martha, we need an emergency replacement of toy bag #113 headed for Maui. And send me a clean uniform too.
Santa: 11:59 PM Dec. 24 from txt

@Santas_twit: Sure thing Kris. Sorry about that.
Martha: 11:59 PM Dec. 24 from web

@S_man_twit: We'll talk about this later.
Santa: 11:59 PM Dec. 24 from txt

@Santas_twit: Ivan, get on it. #NOW
Martha: 11:59 PM Dec. 24 from web

@Toys_r_4_twits: #Wench.
Ivan: 11:59 PM Dec. 24 from web

Ho, Ho, Hey! What Just Happened?

@Santas_twit: Excuse me? #scuseme
Martha: 11:59 PM Dec. 24 from web

@Toys_r_4_twits: Oh, sorry, typo. Meant wrench. Need to bring one. On my way Santa. #rescue
Ivan: 11:59 PM Dec. 24 from web

@Toys_r_4_twits: In the air with Blitzen's youngest, Mini-Blitz. Packed some Dramamine™. ETA: 1 hr 32 min. Ivan to the #rescue.
Ivan: 11:59 PM Dec. 24 from txt

@Santas_twit: Why don't you try to get some rest, Santa.
Martha: 11:59 PM Dec. 24 from web

@S_man_twit: I wreak, Martha. They won't let us off deck, and they're hosing down the reindeer with sea water. What a nightmare. #freezingmybuttoff
Santa: 11:59 PM Dec. 24 from txt

@Toys_r_4_twits: Put that on your #spreadsheet.
Ivan: 11:59 PM Dec. 24 from txt

@Toys_r_4_twits: Have arrived, waiting for clearance to land.
Ivan: 11:59 PM Dec. 24 from txt

@Nimitz_twit: Clearance granted. Land on aft deck next to sleigh.
USS Nimitz: 11:59 PM Dec. 24 from txt

@Toys_r_4_twits: Move over, Rudy. I can't get through. #tightsqueeze
Ivan: 11:59 PM Dec. 24 from txt

Ho, Ho, Hey! What Just Happened?

@I_can_fly_twit: Eat my antlers, if you can reach that
high. #biteme
Rudolph: 11:59 PM Dec. 24 from txt

@S_man_twit: Why are we texting when we are
standing right next to each other?
#stupid
Santa: 11:59 PM Dec. 24 from txt

@Santas_twit: Santa? #hello
Martha: 11:59 PM Dec. 24 from web

@Santas_twit: Anybody? #HELLO
Martha: 11:59 PM Dec. 24 from web

@S_man_twit: Bad news, Martha. Ivan's cell phone fell
in the ocean, and Rudy stepped on his.
Santa: 11:59 PM Dec. 24 from txt

@Santas_twit: Fell in the ocean? #crap
Martha: 11:59 PM Dec. 24 from web

@S_man_twit: Yeah, not sure how that happened.
Reception is bad here. Bars are
disappearing. Must be the radio tower
on the ship. Can't guarantee
communication. #Imfree
Santa: 11:59 PM Dec. 24 from txt

@Santas_twit: Ok, just text me when you get back in
the air. #sigh
Martha: 11:59 PM Dec. 24 from web

@S_man_twit: No can do. Have permission to fly
through restricted air space to make the
flight time shorter. No communication
permitted. Ivan and Mini-Blitz to stay

with me.
Santa: 11:59 PM Dec. 24 from txt

@Santas_twit: But what about my spreadsheet?
Martha: 11:59 PM Dec. 24 from web

@S_man_twit: Stuff the spreadsheet, Martha. Will see
you when we get Home Tweet Home!
#hometweethome
Santa: 11:59 PM Dec. 24 from txt

Ho, Ho, Hey! What Just Happened?

Ho, Ho, Hey! What Just Happened?

Santa and the Fat Farm

Dear Client:

As healthcare insurer for your employer group health plan, we strive to maintain a good working relationship with our clients. We offer a number of programs to keep our members' health at optimum potential so that we can continue to maintain the most cost effective rates across the board.

It has come to our attention that a higher than average number of members for your group have reached the morbidly obese stage. This has caused a significant strain on reimbursement for services directly to your group. As such, we have very limited options.

We have, on your behalf, negotiated a discount rate at a weight management and exercise spa in Arizona. We took the liberty, since it is your off season, to reserve the entire spa for a 30 day period, thus ensuring your total privacy. We require that your group as a whole drop a minimum of 10% body weight, bringing your collective BMI (body mass index) within accepted ranges for your appropriate age group. Failure to comply will result in cancellation of both your health and workers' compensation insurance programs. There is both a human weight loss program, and a veterinary program as well, since we believe that your transportation staff also fall within this unacceptable

Ho, Ho, Hey! What Just Happened?

category. Normally we would have booked transportation for you, however you have air travel available within your organization to utilize at no additional cost, and we believe that the extra trip will do both you and your staff good. In addition, we, having only your best interests at heart, feel that a little more exercise for your staff during the middle of the year, would be an encouragement and a good start toward a healthier and happier lifestyle. We will monitor your success, or lack thereof, while at your stay at the Arizona Fat Reduction Farm so that we may encourage your participation there.

Thank you and have a wonderful time.

Very truly yours,

Your healthcare staff

◊

"They're sending us to a fat farm?"

"Apparently." Santa shifted and loosened his thick black belt. "Ahhh," he said, slouching back against the arm of his easy chair, putting his feet up on a stool.

"But why do all of us have to go?"

Santa looked down at his lead elf and trusted advisor. "Because Ivan, the letter said that we were all overweight."

"Yes, but there's no doubt that most of it is from you. I don't see why we should all be punished."

"There's that team spirit I love to hear."

"Team spirit sucks. I don't want to do this."

"Don't think of it as punishment. Look at it more like a vacation."

Ho, Ho, Hey! What Just Happened?

"A what?"

"A vacation. Something new. Something you've never tried before. Getting away from it all."

"That's funny," Martha said.

"Can't we just fight it instead?" Ivan asked.

"Yes, I plan on doing that, but with less than six months until the busy season starts again, we don't have time to wait and see. We can't go through a Christmas without insurance. It's too high a liability. Pack up the sleigh and hitch the reindeer. I'll make a quick phone call, and we're out of here."

"Where to, sir?"

"Destination, Arizona," Santa said with more than a little depression in his voice.

◊

"Don't stop! Keep on moving." It wasn't so much encouragement as it was an order. "Move! Move! Move!"

"Santa," Ivan gasped, a profuse amount of sweat pouring from his little green brow. "I think I'm going to die."

"If you don't lose weight you'll die," the drill instructor barked from behind his head.

"Keep going," Santa yelled. "Don't stop. She'll attack us again, make us do more."

"I can't do any more. I'm nothing but a huge soaking sponge of sweat." Ivan stopped. "How hot is it? Is there a hospital close? I think I'm having a heart attack."

"110 degrees," she snapped. "Perhaps you could have worn some cooler clothing. I don't think fur-lined wool and knee high boots was a good choice for this weather. Besides, you could all do more if you stopped all this complaining." Amanda marched around in front of the entire group, sizing them up one at a time. "Okay, stop." She stood wide stance, hands on hips, and a nasty glare on her face. "Nobody leaves until we all get serious. Do we *all* understand?"

Santa and the other elves nodded. The reindeer whinnied from the field.

"We have a goal, ladies and gentlemen; a target - a challenge, if you will - that has been set for us all by your sponsors. We will reach that goal! Am I clear?"

They all nodded.

"Good. When we reassemble tomorrow morning at 06:00 I expect 110% from each and every one of you. If not... well, let's just say it won't be an enjoyable day." Amanda turned on her well fit heel, and marched out. As soon as she was out of sight, the room collectively dropped to the floor.

"I can't do this Santa."

"Neither can I."

One elf after another complained. Santa's heart wrenched in his chest. He looked out at the field through the open windows and the stiffeling heat. There, were his beloved reindeer, hitched up to a wagon loaded with bricks and rocks. They were pulling with all of their might, heaving and panting as he had never seen them before.

Santa stood. "Enough is enough!" he said. "I'll be back."

"Where are you going," Mrs. Clause asked, looking up from the floor.

"To make a phone call and get us out of here."

"Oh, no you don't."

Santa shuddered. It was another voice he recognized. Tiffany, their facility assigned counselor.

Santa turned to face her squarely.

"Tiffy," he said curtly.

"Santa."

Ho, Ho, Hey! What Just Happened?

"I need to skip our counseling session today."

"We can't do that now can we? Your insurer's would never allow it."

"Sure we can." He tried to smile at her and turn on the Santa charm, but the twinkle had long since sweated from his eyes. Instead when he cocked his sideways and smiled at her, he looked like he was having a migraine. It hurt too much. He gave up and stood tall.

"This is very important, Tiffany. I have a phone call to make and it can't wait."

"Fine, Santa," she replied. "Even though special arrangements have been made to ensure your privacy, I'll go ahead and report back to our sponsors that you are non-compliant with the program and they can go ahead and cancel your insurance immediately. I don't see any reason to continue this farce."

Santa's face reddened. "You're being very naughty this year, Tiffy. I'm afraid I'm going to have to move you to 'the other list'."

Tiffany smiled. "Whatever you think is best. Shall we get started?" She pointed to a chair. Santa walked over and sat down hard.

"So, tell me now. What are your trigger points?"

"Trigger points?"

"What is it that causes you to overeat? What is the root of the problem?"

"I don't know."

"Oh, but I think you do. Let's dig deeper," she smiled, enjoying herself. "For some it's depression. For others, boredom."

"I'm hardly bored, missy."

"It's Tiffany," she said. "When do you eat the most?"

"Christmas Eve."

"Christmas Eve? Don't most people have their big

meal on Christmas day?"

"Not the milk and cookies," he said. "You see all of my children leave me a little snack when I come to leave their gifts. I have to eat them. It's my way of saying 'thank you'."

"You could leave a note instead."

"It wouldn't be the same."

Tiffany took off her glasses. "Life is all about compromises, Santa. Let's see if we can find one here. The kids all leave you cookies and treats, and you have to be thankful."

He nodded.

She crossed her arms. "Why don't you pack all of the cookies up and load them onto your sleigh in place of the presents you dropped off. You can crumble one up, and pour the milk down the drain so they think you ate them, then drop rest of the cookies off at a local soup kitchen when you make your stop there."

Santa leapt to his feet. "You mean deceive the children!" he shouted. "Lie to them? Make them believe something that isn't true?"

"Calm down, Santa. Parents do it all the time."

"Not parents that expect to get my blessings." He was pacing now. "Don't tell me to calm down when you sit there judging me, telling me to be dishonest and deceitful to my adoring public. Who do you think you are?"

"Sit down, Santa. I'm sure we can come to some kind of understanding here."

"Not with an attitude like that young lady. I don't think we can." Santa marched for the door. "I thought I raised you better than that. We're done."

"This session isn't over until I say it's over," she screamed.

"Whatever, Tiffy!" The big red velvet suit exited the room and the door slammed in his wake. Tiffany looked around at the elves lined up staring at her. "That'll be all for today." She grabbed her clipboard and ran after Santa.

◊

06:00 came bright and early the next morning. Amanda waited for the crew, as usual, outside on the running track. "Late, again." She sighed, shaking her head. Would there be even one single morning she wouldn't have to go roust them from their beds? Grabbing her whistle, she marched toward the dorm rooms.

Bursting into the men's dorm, she flipped on the light and blew the whistle. To her great surprise, there was no movement. She blinked and looked around. The beds were all empty, all still made from the day before. They looked as though none had been slept in. Amanda walked to the window and looked out at the pasture. No reindeer. She turned to go to the reception desk, when a piece of paper on the floor caught her eye. She bent and picked it up. It was a fax.

◊

From: North Pole Law Firm
          Samuel P. Dollingsworth, Esq.
RE: Injunction against North Pole Insurance

Message:

Court ruling in our favor. North Pole Insurance Company has been found to be prejudicial towards persons of excessive weight, and the practice of discriminatory behavior toward same. An immediate injunction has been issued blocking the cancellation of any and all insurance, up to and including both health and workers' compensation policies. In addition, their requirement of 10% collective weight loss in a 30 day period has been found to be excessive based on the AMA® guidelines, and thereby creating an unhealthy and unrealistic weight loss goal, leading the way to other serious health conditions, including but not limited to severe strain on the heart, imbalance of electrolytes, and fatigue. We are to enter into negotiations regarding above issues upon your immediate return to the North Pole.

Congratulations! We won!
Samuel

◊

Amanda sighed. She looked at the fax again. There was handwriting at the bottom. It said:

Amanda and Tiffany. Moved to bad list. Enjoy the coal. Sucks to be you.

S~

Ho, Ho, Hey! What Just Happened?

P.U.K.E. and C.R.A.P. for Animals!

"Ho! Ho! We won't go! Reindeer are people too!"
Splat!

"Martha! What's all that commotion out there?"

"It's those objurgatory protestors again, Santa... Those animal rights people."

"Glad to see you're using the Word-of-the-Day Calendar I gave you last year. Mind telling me what that means now?"

"I don't know, but they're getting louder."

Splat!

Santa jumped backwards. "What in blue blazes is that?"

"Blue what?" Ivan asked.

"Blue Blazes," Martha repeated, looking at the large red slimy spot on her once-beautiful window pane.

"What on earth does that mean?" the head elf asked.

"Forget it," Santa snapped.

"Well, speak English would ya, man. I don't know what all this objiggy blue garbage means."

"*For-get-it*," Santa said again, a little shorter than he had intended. "Let's just figure out who these people are, and how to get rid of them."

Splat! Splat! Crash!

Ho, Ho, Hey! What Just Happened?

This assault broke the window to the front room where they all stood. There was a collective "EWWW!" as the rancid odor wafted through the broken glass and into the warmth of the living quarters.

"Rotten tomatoes!"

"Ok, that does it," Santa snapped. "I'm going out there!"

"You can't do that," his wife protested.

"Sure I can. It's what they want."

"But you don't even know who they are," she said.

Santa looked out the window. There, at the end of his driveway were a couple of dozen people pacing and carrying signs. One sign read:

P.U.K.E. for Animals

And the other read:

C.R.A.P. Right Now!

"Have you ever heard of either of them before?" Martha asked, as her husband moved toward the front door.

"No, but when they find out I am about to take names and move them to the Naughty List, I guarantee they'll high tail it out of here, and take all their P.U.K.E. and C.R.A.P. with them!" Santa yanked the front door open and stepped out into the bright sunlight.

Splat! Splat! Splat!

Three rapid fire tomatoes hit their target, forcing the rotund red man to retreat back into his house.

"Ewww!!! You stink!"

"Get out, Santa. You're stinking up my house!" Martha ordered.

The elves all covered their noses, and Ivan started to gag and wretch in the corner.

"I didn't think you could ever be any more red or

revolting, but I was wrong," Martha said. "Get out! You're horrid!"

She covered her mouth and nose with her apron, closed her tearing eyes, and shoved her husband hard toward the door. Ivan, head elf, slammed it behind him.

Splat!

"Ok," Santa yelled down the driveway, "I'm coming down- - -"

Splat!

Head shot...

" - - - to talk about whatever - - -"

Splat!

In the hair...

"Hey, look now. I'm out here trying - - -"

Splat! Splat!

In the mouth and up the nose...

Santa gagged and spit on the lawn. He took a deep breath and regained his composure and turned back to the street.

"I've had enough! You people knock it off before I - - -"

Splat! Splat! Crash!

Santa turned his back for cover, just in time to see another broken window pane, with his wife and staff glaring at him from inside his once peaceful sanctuary. Santa sighed. This was going to be a long afternoon.

He stood for a minute weighing his options. They would not attack his back. They wanted full frontal humiliation. He unbuttoned his custom red velvet jacket and stripped it off, dropping it on the ground, stained with a foul stench. Off came his white undershirt next, leaving him donning his comfortable grey long johns with the holes in them. He raised the white t-shirt over his head and flew it in surrender, then turned slowly to face the crowd. The driveway people cheered as though they had just won the Super Bowl. Santa proceeded with caution down the drive to meet with his tormentors. He heard "atta, boy," and "teach 'em a lesson" from his loved ones behind him, but kept his eyes forward, locked on his adversaries ahead.

♪♫♪ Home ♪,♫ Home, on the range. ♪♫♫ Where the reindeer ♫ and the antelope play ♫♫♪♫...NOT!

"Santa's reindeer don't get to play anywhere!" one man yelled. "They're beasts of burden, forced to work long hours and pull loads that far exceed their weight bearing capacity - all the while eating nothing but carrots." He waved a carrot menacingly toward Santa as he arrived at the bottom of the driveway. "Can you tell me Santa, why is it that you get cookies and milk, eggnog, and whatever else people like to leave for you, but the reindeer get nothing but carrots?"

"Ahhhh. I, um- - -" Santa was dumbfounded. He had never considered what others were leaving for his staff before.

"Well, fat man? Have an answer?"

"I don't really have any control over what other people do."

"What?" the man screamed. "One word from you and the whole world listens! Why don't you just tell them that reindeer like a little variety too! How would you like to eat nothing but carrots for the longest, hardest night of your life? They're not obese like you. Maybe you should try eating nothing but carrots. Maybe you could trim down a little, huh?"

"Ok, Sam," another man stepped in. "We have a lot of issues to discuss."

"None of them more important than this one!" Sam shot back.

"I beg your pardon," the C.R.A.P. ladies chimed in, "but false imprisonment and deplorable conditions are important too."

"What?" Santa said, stunned.

"Yeah, you heard me," the smallest of the ladies bellowed out. "And don't pretend like you don't know what I'm talking about." Her grey head bobbled around on her shoulders like a dime store toy.

"I'm sure I don't," Santa said. "Nobody's in prison here."

"Oh?" she asked her accusatory tone unmistakable. "And how about all those little kittens and puppies that you shove into tiny cages?"

"Those cages are for their safety, so they won't fall out of the sleigh mid-flight. They run free until Christmas Eve, I assure you."

"They're prison cells!" she screamed, "and you're the warden. What have those innocent little animals ever done to you? They don't deserve this treatment. You have violated their civil rights and we intend to see you punished for it!"

"Civil rights?" Santa said. "You can't be serious."

"Oh, I assure you I am very serious, mister. You drug them against their will and throw them into cages for days on end."

"Now wait just a minute," Santa snapped back. "They get Dramamine™ for the long flight so they don't puke in the sleigh," he smiled at the irony of the word 'puke'. "And, as for being in the cages for long periods, everyone knows that on Christmas night time stands still so they don't even know how long they're in there. To them it seems only like a few short minutes, during which they are all asleep."

"Yeah, it's a lot easier just to drug them all isn't it? You're nothing a filthy drug dealer lowlife!" she shouted back.

"Where are you from again, princess?"

"C.R.A.P.," she said proudly. "Claustrophobic Release the Animals Program."

"C.R.A.P. Right Now!" the people behind her

Ho, Ho, Hey! What Just Happened?

started shouting. "C.R.A.P. Right Now!"

"Ok. Ok, people. Let's all just calm down," the man in charge said. He turned to look at Santa. "I'm the head of the local P.U.K.E. chapter," he said handing Santa a business card.

Santa looked down. The card read:

P.U.K.E.
People Urgently Keeping Ethics
North Pole Chapter
Hearl Itall, President

"Hurl?" Santa asked.

"It's pronounced Earl. The H is silent."

"Hurl It All?" Santa asked again.

"That's I-tall, emphasis on the I" Hearl shot back angrily.

"Very well, Mr. Hurl It All, what can I do for you?"

"We're here on behalf of the reindeer and other animals that have no voices of their own. Someone has to protect them so they are not abused and forced to do things that they don't want to do. That's our job," he finished, head held high.

"You've obviously never met MY reindeer." Santa smirked.

"I don't find any of this amusing, mister. Are you willing to negotiate with us or not? We can make your life miserable if we have to."

"Yeah, I'm feeling it already," Santa said. "Exactly what is it you want me to do?"

Here is our list of demands:

1. For the sleigh, use only organic, free-range reindeer. When in the off season, the reindeer are allowed to run free on the range or wherever they wish. A

P.U.K.E. volunteer is to be placed on staff for the night of Christmas Eve to ensure that the animals are treated well and have sufficient breaks and proper meals.

2. Santa is to put the word out to his adoring public that Reindeer are undulates and survive on more than carrots. Their main diet consists of green plants, moss, fungus and algae. They love apples with the skin on, and have been known to eat small animals and fish. They also like the occasional sweet treats as well. Santa will share the cookies that have been left for him with his other staff and not selfishly keep them all to himself.

3. Eating only carrots leaves the reindeer malnourished and ill equipped to pilot the massive and overloaded sleigh. The animals are distressed and severely strained, leaving the door open for mid air collisions or pilot error, mistakes that could be costly in lives and human hurt. Billions of people would be left toyless on Christmas morning due to Santa's thoughtlessness and careless behavior. FAA regulations clearly state, and I quote: *'Current FAA regulations for domestic flights generally limit pilots to eight hours of flight time during a 24-hour period. This limit may be extended provided the pilot receives additional rest at the end of the flight. However, a pilot is not allowed to accept, nor is an airline allowed to assign, a flight if the pilot has not had at least eight continuous hours of rest during the 24-hour period.'* The FAA will be immediately be notified that the reindeer are out of compliance with this regulation. The FAA will further be on alert for every Christmas to make sure that the regulations are strictly adhered to.

4. To make a point of what he has cruelly put his reindeer through, Santa and his entire crew must go vegetarian for one entire Christmas season . This includes the toy-making season as well as delivery (definition of a season = 1 full year). They must also encourage the public not to have turkey or ham for their Christmas dinners as well. Millions of turkeys can be spared by this one simple gesture. Tofu-rkey makes a great a great alternative.

5. Animals reserved for delivery as pets are no longer to be placed in cages, nor drugged to keep them from vomiting. They are to have their own attendants, and alternative delivery systems established if their safety in the sleigh cannot be guaranteed.

6. Santa and his crew must volunteer in the off season at the P.U.K.E. headquarters so that he can better understand the unique needs of the animals and learn better how to care for them.

"We'll give you some time to think about our demands," Hearl said, folding his papers and stuffing them back into his pockets.

"No, that won't be necessary," Santa said. "I can give you my answers right now."

"First of all, there is no such thing as forcing a reindeer to do anything that they don't want to do. They are very stubborn creatures, and have minds of their own. They are also much larger than I am. They already roam free whenever and wherever they want to, so that is a moot point. There are no 'reindeer breeding mills.' They all come from the wild, and therefore, are by definition, organic and free-range."

Ho, Ho, Hey! What Just Happened?

Sam bristled.

"As far as them starving on just carrots, I think you will have a hard time convincing anybody, including a civil rights judge, that a 2000 pound animal is starving, but if you want them to eat more than carrot sticks, I will put the word out. They can eat anything that they want as far as I'm concerned, so long as it doesn't give them gas. Mexican food is out. On top of that, since you have never examined them personally, or seen the conditions that we operate in on Christmas Eve, your accusations are pure conjecture here. Show me some proof."

"We can't," Sam responded. "We tried to get sub-rosa films, but the photographer kept falling asleep. Did you drug him too?"

"That's the magic of Christmas," Santa said. "All of the world's brats fall asleep and stay asleep so I can get some work done. No one undesirable can stay awake."

"Are you going to go vegetarian?" Hearl demanded, changing the subject.

"Sure."

"For a whole year?"

"Why not? If it will get you people out of here, I'll do it. Besides, how hard can it be? I love veggies. But I am not eating Tofu-rkey. I hate Tofu."

"Fine," Hearl said. "We can get the word out on that another way. We'll advertize."

"As far as flight times go, you can call the FAA if you like, but to them, the time frame of Christmas Eve is a normal night. They will see nothing unusual or out of the ordinary, so go ahead. Call them. Also, as a matter of legal fact, reindeer are not pilots, therefore the pilot restrictions do not apply. I will also *not* have one of your P.U.K.E. people in my restricted warehouse looking through the presents before delivery. That is a security warehouse and your people do not have clearance. They will not be permitted inside."

"We'll picket!"

"Go ahead. No one will be awake to see you. What else was on your list?"

"Delivery system for pets," the C.R.A.P. lady shouted.

"Ahhh yes, this I am definitely willing to compromise on. I am tired of having the little hairballs hurl in my sleigh," Santa said. Then he looked at Hearl. "No pun intended."

"It's Earl. The H is silent."

"Yes, I heard. I am willing to have them delivered by courier, but with the increased costs and added delivery schedules, some requests will not be able to be approved. The first one would be yours, princess," he said looking at the C.R.A.P. lady. "The kitten you asked for will be denied this year.

She broke into tears and ran, leaving Santa to face the rest of the crowd.

"And as far as me volunteering in your offices, you can all just kiss-off. There's no way I would ever voluntarily walk into your establishments. It would take a judge and an armed police officer to get me in there. You people should be ashamed of the way that you - - -"

Splat!

Santa grimaced at a blow from yet another tomato. As he opened his mouth to speak, another onslaught began.

Splat! Splat! Splat!

But, this one wasn't at him. This one was from behind. He turned to see a tiny green regiment of vegetably armed elves, little arms cocked and ready for battle. Behind them were nine extremely large and angry reindeer.

"Look," Sam said. "We're just trying to bring some issues to the- - -"

Ho, Ho, Hey! What Just Happened?

Splat! Sam touched his wet face.

The army moved closer.

"Wow. The reindeer are a lot bigger than I - - -"

Splat! Splat!

"Hey now! Wait a minute." Sam wiped the slimy tomato skins from his face. "We're not the bad guys here. We are just protecting- -"

"Elves protect the animals!" Ivan yelled. "Get 'em!"

The tiny green army lurched forward and fired at once, pelting the crowd with tomatoes, carrot sticks, and slimy onion peels of their own.

Santa turned and slowly walked back toward his house, leaving the ruckus behind him. The elves didn't get much entertainment in the off season. They deserved a little fun. After all, they were the ones who cared for all those animals. Accusations of abuse were very personal to them. Reaching the porch, he looked back at the green flash chasing the protestors down the street. Santa smiled.

"I am in charge of Christmas," he hollered down the driveway. "-Emphasis on the I."

"Very clever, Santa", Martha said plugging her nose. "Now get in the shower and get all that P.U.K.E. and C.R.A.P. off you."

Ho, Ho, Hey! What Just Happened?

Twenty Nine Minutes

"How long do you think this will take?"

"You mean how long will she last?" Donner asked. "I don't know. Doesn't look very tough," he said looking at Blitzen. "The last one was gone in less than a day."

"We can do better than that," Rudolph chimed in.

"Are we shooting for a new record? I say less than 30 minutes."

"That's pretty aggressive, Blitz. What do you have in mind?"

"Nothing, Rudy, honest." He smiled.

"Well, realistically, I think we can shoot for noon. That would be half a day." Donner looked at the clock on the wall.

"I still say less than 30, and if I win, then I get to lead the sleigh," Blitzen said. "Just like I used to before you and your shiny little snout came along."

"Ok, as long as it isn't storming. Santa would have my hide otherwise."

"I'll take care of Santa. Let's just take care of this first."

"Ok, boys," a woman's voice broke in. "Let's all gather round. We're all here for an exciting day of obedience training! My name is Chastity, and I have treats for everyone. Oh, and my friends all call me Chas."

Ho, Ho, Hey! What Just Happened?

"Treats, oh boy!" Blitzen charged the trainer, knocking her off her feet, his head shoved into the treat bag.

"Chastity? That's cute. Think it's true?" Cupid asked.

"Boys?" Vixen said. "So only the *boys* are invited to have treats? This sucks. I'm leaving. Let's go Cupid."

"Oh, I'm so sorry girlfriends," Chas said from the ground. "Come on over here." The trainer stood and put her arms out to give her new friends a big hug. Vixen backed up, snorting. "Ok, no hugging just yet. I understand. You don't know me," Chas told them both. "But, I guarantee by the end of this day we are all going to be good friends!"

"If you're such a good friend you'd pass out those treats you just promised," Donner yelled.

"Well, unfortunately, Blitzen has just devoured them all, but we can still have some fun without- - -"

All nine reindeer turned to leave.

"No, wait. I can get some more," she said. "I'll get some more. Give me a few minutes."

"Yeah, come back when you have some pay dirt, lady."

"Not a problem Donner. I'll send my assistant to the store to get more Milk Bones™."

"Dog treats?" Dancer said, pure disgust in his voice. "You brought us dog treats?"

"Why yes, Dancer. They're very healthy, made from- - -"

"I'm Dasher," he interrupted.

"I'm Dancer," she heard from behind.

"Oh, I'm so sorry. I thought I had all of your pictures memorized. I won't make that mistake again." She studied their faces. "Dasher and Dancer. Got it."

"What about the treats?" Prancer shouted.

Ho, Ho, Hey! What Just Happened?

"Well, as I said, my assistant will go to the store to get some more- - -"

"Better not be dog treats."

"- - more, - - more treats" she stuttered. "What would you all like? How about some nice carrots?"

"How about some nice carrots, she wants to know?" Comet began to circle her, snorting, agitation growing with each step. "How about some nice carrots? Do you know what it's like to eat nothing but carrots from stop to stop on the longest night of your life?" His pace increased as he inched closer to Chastity. "And, to leave them uneaten would be an insult to every child on this planet. So, in order to be the nice, well-trained, thoughtful, considerate reindeer that we are," he said, only inches from her face now, "you eat every single stinking carrot, stop after stop, city after city, country after country, continent after continent! Is that what you're asking us? How about some nice carrots?" He was screaming now, the force of his breath blowing her hair away from her face as he loomed down over her.

"Wh-, wh-," she swallowed hard. "What would you like to have?"

Comet backed up. "I don't know. Hey guys, what would we all like to have?" Voice happy as a clam now.

"I want what Santa gets." Cupid stood in the background.

"Oh, cookies and milk?" Chastity answered.

"Oh you poor, ignorant thing." Vixen shook her head.

"What? That's what I always left Santa."

"And that's why you never got any of the things that you asked for either, honey." Blitzen was the one pacing now. "Other people left prime rib dinners with potatoes au gratin."

"They did?"

"Yes, and vegetable medley's with hollandaise

sauce," he added.

"For Santa?"

"Yes, for Santa. Why do you think he struggles with his weight so much?" Blitzen moved in close. "Do you ever use the brain inside that blonde bubble of yours?"

"Well, I guess I never thought about it before," Chastity said, tears welling up. "That's why I never got what I asked for?" she said, crying.

"There's a lot you never thought about, honey. Like being alone with nine starving reindeer that weigh well over 2,000 pounds." Donner was angry now. He turned and winked at Rudolph.

"Yeah, where are those treats?" Rudolph glared at her.

"Jason, bring some prime rib as soon as you can please," Chas said, standing in the bright red glare of two flared nostrils. There was just the faintest hint of a quiver in her voice.

"And," Blitzen prodded, the fuzz on this antlers ticking the tip of her nose.

"And potatoes au gratin."

"And,?"

"Vegetable medley with hollandaise sauce, please. As fast as you can."

"Ice cream," Cupid said. "I want ice cream."

"Oh, with chocolate sauce," Vixen added.

"Oh yes! Chocolate sauce too." Cupid giggled. "How could I forget that? Everything's better when you smear a little chocolate on it."

Blitzen giggled back at Vix and bobbed his head. "You got that one right." Vixen blushed.

Chastity nodded toward her assistant who jumped into his car and sped off toward the closest store.

"What should we all do now?" Rudolph asked.

"Let's play some reindeer games." Comet was

jumping. "Please?"

"No, we can't do that." Chastity folded her arms across her chest and took a firm stance.

"Why not?"

"Because reindeer games are sexist and exclusionary. They are not fair to everyone, so no one should be allowed to participate. Besides, we are here for some mandatory obedience training ordered by the North Pole Animal Control District, not to play games." Chastity addressed the group head on. "We, myself included, don't approve of competitive games."

"Oh, and why do you feel that way?" Donner demanded.

"Well," she said, clearing her throat. "Studies of school aged children have shown that if all students are not given equal odds to achieve the same goals, then they have lower self esteem and tend to get lower grades in school. We feel- - -"

"We?" Rudolph questioned.

"Yes, my organization, and I-, I-, I-," she stuttered. "My organization and I. We believe in equal opportunity for all. Everyone should be given an equal chance to succeed, even if we have to make the odds more in their favor."

"So, let me get this straight, sugar," Donner said. "You feel that the younger and smaller members of the herd should be given the same chance to lead Santa's sleigh as the older, stronger members of the team."

"Yes, exactly. My name is Chastity, not sugar."

"And what if we get caught in a snow storm, and they are not strong enough to get the rest of us out?" he asked. "Do we all die knowing that they had a fair and equal chance to feel better about themselves?"

"Well, what are the odds of that happening, really?"

"Pretty stinking high lady. Do you remember

what night of the year we are out on? And not for us. We're out there risking our lives for you people."

"I don't want to lead the sleigh," Vixen said. "I can't do it. It's too heavy. I prefer to give Blitz directions."

"Oh, don't tell her that!" Blitzen yelled. "You said you'd never tell anyone!"

"Sorry Blitz."

"Now everyone's going to tease me."

"Nobody's going to tease you, honey," Vixen said. "I just want her to know that everyone is different. We all have special gifts and talents. I can't pull the heavy weight of a sleigh, and you can't find your way out of a paper bag in a snow storm."

"Vix! Come on!"

"Wait," Chas paused. "Are you two?"

"What's it to ya?" Blitzen charged.

"Nothing," Chas said, backing away. "Nothing."

"Reindeer games are the only way that we can identify what our own unique gifts are." The fuzz on Blitzen's antlers was tickling her nose her nose again.

"Show me," she said, hoping to get the reindeer to back away a little from her.

"Launch!" Donner screamed.

In an instant they were all airborne, ascending to heights she never thought possible. They flew in perfect formation, rounding her position over and over again. Just watching them made her dizzy. One by one they all began to slow, and then land next to her, heaving and panting from the exhaustion. Dang! Surrounded again.

"You see, we all have our strengths," Donner pointed out. "The strongest lead. We hold up the others with our sheer strength and size. The rest lean on us when they are not able to stand. There are four of us; Donner, Blitzen, Dasher, Comet."

"Dancer and Prancer are the comic relief," Donner

took over. "They keep us laughing and our moods light as we get through the longest, toughest night of the year."

Comet stepped up. "Vixen and Cupid are the brains. They plan the route and get us there. Nature's GPS. There's no one better. The team depends on them, although some refuse to admit it." He laughed at Blitzen.

"Only one lights the way to see us through the darkest storms," Vixen said. "He's the only one that can. That's Rudolph, although we try not to tell him that. He gets a big nose when he thinks he's important."

"Organized games are how we see who is a good fit and who is not," Cupid said. "They are the glue that holds us all together. The Olympic games are not handicapped so everyone gets an equal chance to win. Only those strong enough and with the right skills can survive."

"You see," Vixen said. "We are not all the same."

"Yes," Chas interrupted, "but the studies have proven."

"Screw your studies, sugar. Let's see what your talents are." Donner moved in close again.

"Oh, no thank you. I have a bad back."

"Oh, no, sugar. Wouldn't hear of skipping you, Everyone deserves a fair and equal chance. Go ahead, fly."

"I can't fly."

"Sure you can. We are all the same. Go ahead." Donner lowered his head and gave her a rough shove with his large snout. She took a header and landed face first in the dirt.

"Now, now. Let's not be mean," Blitz said. "She's just a human. She can't fly."

"Thank you, Vixen." Chas tried to brush the dirt off her clothing, to no avail.

Ho, Ho, Hey! What Just Happened?

"I'm Prancer. Geez, you can't even get the sex right."

"I'm sorry," Chas said, standing up again. "I didn't mean - - -"

"Yeah, yeah. Ok. She can't fly," Prancer said. "Let's just have her pull the sleigh instead."

"I can't pull that! It must weigh 2,500 pounds."

"3,650 pounds, empty, to be exact," Prancer smiled down at her. "But remember, we are all the same."

"That's with adjustments," Chastity protested. "Each person would get a handicap to give them a fair and equal chance."

"Sure thing, sugar," Prancer said. "We'll just get you a smaller sleigh, and then tell half the kids in the world that they don't get any presents this year so you can feel better about yourself."

"No, that's not what I- - -"

"Well, sure it is!" Prancer turned to face her head on. "You want to lull everyone into a false sense of security of thinking that they can do anything, then when they get out into the real world and find out they can't, you want the world to make adjustments to accommodate them, rather than the other way around. Read your history books lady."

"My history books?"

"Yeah. How many Martin Luther King Jr.'s were there?" he asked.

"One."

"Abraham Lincoln? Mother Theresa? Princess Diana? What about Moses, or Jesus?"

"Well, only one," she said. "What's your point?"

"Do you know why?" All of the reindeer rounded on her now. "Because they were special. No one else could do what they did, or be them, no matter how much they want to. Each of us has our own place in this

Ho, Ho, Hey! What Just Happened?

world, and we, alone, have to find it. Not make it up as we go, or change the odds to make us into something that we can't be otherwise. So go ahead," they pushed her hard again, "pull the sleigh."

Reins and a harness were thrown unceremoniously over her head. They were so heavy she could barely stand under their weight.

"I don't think this is a good- - -"

"PULL!" they screamed.

She lunged forward with all her might, but the sleigh did not budge. Behind her, Chastity could hear reindeer laughter. She sat down to cry.

"Get up, Princess," Vixen said. "It's not break time yet.

"I can't do this," she cried. "It's too heavy."

"No whining now, sugar," Donner said. "Believe me, you don't want to be on the 'naughty' list. Stand up."

She stood again, protesting, still crying. The female reindeer took pity on her and decided to help her.

"PULL!" Donner screamed again.

Chastity lunged forward again with all her might. Cupid and Vixen lunged forward too. The sleigh lurched forward and Chas flew face down into the dirt for the second time. She once again burst into tears.

"Stop!" she cried. "We have to finish our training. It's been ordered. What am I supposed to tell the Animal Control District?"

"Tell them that by order of the local P.U.K.E. and C.R.A.P. chapters, we are organic, free-range reindeer, and therefore are not subject to their rules and regulations. They can take their orders and stuff it," Donner said. "You can too, Chastity."

"You are the meanest animals I have ever seen in my life," she screamed. "I hate you all!"

"Yeah, right back at 'cha, honey." Rudolph

laughed. The others joined in.

"I mean it," Chas went on. "In all my life I have never met a more rowdy, untrained, obnoxious group of - -, of- - "

"Of what, Princess?" Vixen teased. "Animals? Wild animals?"

"I- - -, I- - -" She broke off again and turned to run, forgetting she still had the reins around her neck.

"Strike three!" Comet laughed as Chastity hit the dirt for the third time. "You're out!"

"Jacob!" she screamed as she saw her assistant arriving with the meal.

"Let's eat!" Vixen said. "I'm starving. That was hard work."

"Time?" Rudolph asked.

"29 minutes," Donner said, "a new record."

"I win!" Blitzen screamed. "I win. I win. I win. I get to lead the sleigh again!"

"Only if Santa allows it," Rudolph protested, "And only if it's not storming."

"Yeah, yeah. Whatever. ♫ I get to lead the sleigh.♪ ♫ I get to lead the sleigh.♫♫ Dang, we're good!"

"Next time we're gonna need a stop watch!" Rudolph's nose was glowing.

"Hey, Vix, launch some of that food over here, would ya?" Donner said. "Let's celebrate! I'm starving."

"Here ya go Don," Vixen said, laughing. "Here's a nice big Milk Bone™."

♪ ♫ Do You Smell What I Smell? ♫♫♪

North Pole Bail Bonds. How can I help you?"

"No one can ever know about this!"

"Try and relax, Mr. Clause. We do this all the time."

"Yeah, but not for Santa! If word got out that I was busted for a DUI my reputation would be ruined."

"Sir, word won't get out from us, but you have to understand that arrest documents are public record. Anyone can go to the courthouse and get copies of anything at any time." Alex looked at his watch. It was getting late. "It's nearly midnight now. Shall we get started?"

"Yes, let's. I'm in kind of a hurry, as you can imagine."

"Why don't you tell me what happened."

"Well, first of all, it's not my fault," Santa said.

"Of course not. It never is."

"What's that supposed to mean?"

"It means," Alex said, "that the police can't pull you over for no reason. There had to be something that gave you away to them."

"They didn't pull me over. I fell on them."

"You fell on them?" he asked. "How did that happen?"

"Well, me and the reindeer, we were up on the rooftop, you know, click, click, click."

"Yes, I know the song. What happened then?"

"It was an A-frame house so the pitch was really

steep. Ivan, my lead elf forgot to pack the chains again, so we had no traction. I came back up the chimney after delivering the presents. Old Rudolph takes a step aside to give me some more room, and the whole sleigh starts to slide backwards."

"Sleighs can do that?"

"Sure they can. It's not magic, you know. Slick tread on an icy roof means disaster no matter what you're driving. Anyway, it took all the reindeer by surprise, moving backwards like that. None of 'em saw it coming. So off the roof we slide like a wet piece of cheese. That's when we hit them."

"The police car?" Alex asked.

"Yeah, the cops. Apparently someone called in a prowler in the neighborhood so they were out checking on things."

"Go on," Alex said, pushing his chair back and putting his feet up on the desk. He checked his watch. Nearly midnight.

"That's when things got messy."

"Messy?"

"They said I had all these violations on my VE-HICLE, something about broken or missing brake lights and turn signals. Then they wanted me to take some kind of a test."

"Sobriety test?" Alex asked.

"Yeah, that was it. Anyway, I said no. They can't make me take any test, I'm in a hurry. I have things to do. They said if I didn't take the test they would take me and the entire crew in. Said belligerent something or other too."

"So you refused the sobriety test?"

"I didn't refuse, I just wanted to know why I had to take it and nobody else did. There were nine reindeer and three elves in the sleigh with me, and people lining up on the street by this time to watch. Why didn't any of them have to take the stupid test?"

"What did the police say?"

"They said they could smell me. Can you imagine! How rude is that? Didn't their mother's raise them with any kind of manners at all?"

"Santa, if they could smell the alcohol on you that's not a good thing."

"They couldn't smell me. It was all a set-up, a shake down just to get better presents. I didn't buy it."

"I can smell you from here. What have you been drinking?"

"Just the egg nog that people leave out for me, like every year. Hey! I didn't do anything wrong!" Santa protested. "Do you know what would happen if I didn't eat and drink everything that people leave out for me? You'd think that people would learn by now. How hard is it to figure out they would have a tipsy Santa if they left out booze? But no! They don't. Leave one snack uneaten and people get mad. Mix up a present and the hate mail comes in. Skip a house, or a country, and the whole world wants to crucify you! I'm damned if I do, and damned if I don't? What's a Santa to do?"

"I don't really know the answer to that," Alex said.

"So then I guess my wife called you on her cell phone to bail me out, and here we are."

"Here we are," Alex said, sitting back up straight in his chair.

"So what now?" Santa asked. "I have deliveries to make and reindeer to feed."

"Well, your wife put down a deposit and collateral against your bail, so we were able to get you out. That's the good news."

Santa nodded. "What's the bad news?"

"Your sleigh has been impounded and the lot won't be open until the morning." Alex looked at his watch. "It's nearly midnight now. I suggest you get some sleep and we can get your sleigh released in the morning."

"That's no good. This is Christmas Eve. I need my sleigh tonight or Christmas will be ruined. We need to get it out."

"What you need to do is to go somewhere quiet and sleep it off. Things will look a whole lot better in the morning."

"I can't do that. I need to get back on the road."

"The sleigh and your reindeer are behind an eight-foot barbed wire fence right now. There's no getting to them."

"That's not a problem," Santa smiled. "The reindeer are very nimble. Besides, I have to be in Europe by midnight."

"That's not going to happen," Alex said gruffly. "Let me explain something to you, Santa. You're in a lot of trouble right now. You are facing some daunting legal troubles. You will have to appear before a judge, you could lose your driver's license, and possibly do some jail time for this. A DUI is nothing to take lightly. You will get points on your DMV record, your insurance will skyrocket, if it isn't cancelled completely.

"I don't actually have a driver's license so I don't think they can take it away from me. I have health insurance already, so that shouldn't matter, although they have already told me they think I am out of shape and need to lose some weight. That was pretty rude too, if you ask me. They're already on the naughty list."

"Look, Santa. You're in a lot of trouble with the law already, and that doesn't even include me."

"You? What are you talking about, Alex? I thought you were here to help me."

"I *am* here to help you, but let me make something completely clear. If you skip on me and try to flee to another country, I will send out my bounty hunters after you to drag your sorry drunken butt right back here. And then I will take great pleasure in sending you back to jail. Don't even try that garbage on me. Do you understand?"

Santa swallowed hard. "Yes, Alex, I do understand. What is the next step?"

"Like I said, I suggest that you go find a quiet place to sleep it off. We can meet back here at 8:00 in the morning and we can formulate a plan then. Based on what you've told me I think you have a chance to get off."

"Get off?"

"Yes, get off on the charges."

"How's that?"

"Well, you weren't actually driving at the time, you were sliding. The law states *Driving Under the Influence.* You weren't technically *driving* from what you have related to me."

"That's right! I wasn't. I was *Sliding Under the Influence.* Is there a law against that?"

"No. Just public drunkenness, but that's not what they charged you with."

"Excellent, and now you want me to get some rest?"

"Yes, I do," Alex said again.

"Good. Good. I can do that. Actually, I think that is a good idea. I will meet you back here at 8:00 a.m. on December 25th, right?"

"Yes, that's right."

"And what time is it now?"

Alex looked at his watch. "Almost midnight. Try to get some rest, Santa."

"Absolutely, Alex. I can guarantee that I will be well rested before I come back in the morning. Which way is the impound lot?"

Ho, Ho, Hey! What Just Happened?

"I already old you that the sleigh will stay there until the morning when the police release it. I will go with you to get it out then."

"Yes, yes, of course," Santa said. "I just want to make sure the reindeer are well fed and taken care of."

"Am I going to get another call from the police tonight about you, Santa?"

"Why, no," Santa smiled. "What do you think I'm gonna do, bust the reindeer free and run with them?"

"You'd better not!"

"I know, I know. Bounty hunters dragging my drunken butt. I remember. I just want to make sure that my staff is taken care of before I go to sleep. I have legal obligations here. They are in my employ."

"Uh huh." Alex looked skeptical.

"Look," Santa said. "You already said they were surrounded by an eight-foot barbed wire fence. They would have to fly to get out of there. Do you really believe that, at your age? I'm surprised at you."

Alex sighed. He raised a finger and pointed down the block. "Impound is down two streets and to the left. If I hear one more thing before 8:00 am - - -"

"You won't!" Santa promised. "I guarantee that you won't. Have a great Christmas morning, Alex. Enjoy that present that you're getting too. I know you've been waiting for it for a long time."

Alex turned to leave. "This is going to be a long night."

"You have no idea!" Santa shot back heading down the block, then he stopped. "Hey, can I ask you something?" he yelled back to Alex. "Answer me honestly."

Alex nodded.

"Do I really smell?"

Ho, Ho, Hey! What Just Happened?

To Be or to Beano™
That is the Question

"Can I help you sir?"

"It wasn't my fault."

"Excuse me?"

"Moron had to go and check everything on the stupid thing."

"Sir, do you need help with your car?"

"The VE-HICLE, the man said. Anybody can see it's not a car."

"Of course not. Do you need some help with your vehicle?" The mechanic shifted, uncomfortable behind the counter.

"They leave it out for me. What would happen if I didn't drink it? What would people do then?"

"Huh?"

"How would you feel?"

"I don't know."

"Exactly. You plan all year long. You get your hopes up and then some insensitive selfish wanna-be takes a dump all over your dreams. It would be a revolt, that's what. Do you think I had a choice?" Santa demanded. "People have expectations. I have to live up to it. Nobody asked me if I wanted it."

"Sir, do you need something?"

"Well I think we established that when I walked into your shop, didn't we?" Santa turned and rolled his eyes at Ivan through the window of the smog station.

Ho, Ho, Hey! What Just Happened?

"What exactly can I do for you, sir?"

"I need an emergency smog check to register my VE-HICLE and to fight the DUI that idiot arrested me for." Santa shook his head. "And to think of all the presents I left for his kids. And him too."

"Sir, you don't really fight a DUI with a smog certificate."

"There was some other stuff too. Hey, do you fix tail lights?"

"Yes, sir."

"I think I need one of those too."

"Certainly. Which side?"

"Ah- - , both. Don't actually haven any. What's a turn signal?"

Santa's question was met with nothing but a blank stare.

"Hey, I don't usually get much traffic where I drive."

"Of course, what is the make and model of your car?"

"VE-HICLE."

"Yes, of course. The VE-HICLE."

Santa turned to leave.

"Sir?"

"You wouldn't believe me if I told you. Wait here. I'll drive it in."

◊

The mechanic walked over and grabbed a long metal probe. "Where's the tailpipe?" he asked holding it up high.

Rudolph squealed and jerked backward, landing his tail right into Donner's head.

"Hey, watch it!" the senior undulate grumbled.

"Sorry," Rudolph said, still refusing to move

forward.

"Give me that" Santa snapped, reaching for the instrument. "I'll just hold it back here."

"Normally we don't have anyone in the driver's seat when we test cars- -, I mean vehicles," the mechanic said.

"Well you normally don't test sleigh's either, do you Smarty Marty?"

"Don't call me that!"

"Why? That's how you used to sign your letters telling me how to deliver all my presents so you could get yours faster. Do you remember that?"

"Yes, sir," Martin answered, head hanging a little low.

"Let's just get on with it, if you don't mind. I'm in kind of a hurry."

"Yes, sir," Martin said again. "We'll need to get the sleigh up to 100 mph." He reached over and turned a knob on the wall.

The ramp under their feet lurched into motion and the reindeer began running, speed increasing rapidly. Santa held the reins and tried to keep his team from sliding off the runners. He had the reins tight in one hand and the tailpipe probe in the other.

"Come on, guys," he yelled. "Let's get this together, would ya? You look like a bunch of teenage track runners. Get in sync!"

Struggling to keep up, barely able to stay on the track, Donner was the first to relent. "Launch!" he yelled as the team took flight in the garage.

"They're flying! They're Flying!" Smarty Marty screamed.

"They're reindeer, genius!" Santa yelled back. "It's what they do."

"They can't," Martin yelled, grabbing Rudolph's reins. "It'll screw up the test."

Ho, Ho, Hey! What Just Happened?

"Tie them down!" Santa yelled, "or we're all doomed!"

Martin turned and tied the reins down to the nearest heavy object he could find, a Volkswagen™. It immediately began to skid sideways through the garage toward the smog check area.

"Yeee Hawww!" Santa yelled, as though he were atop a bucking bronco. "How long will this take?" he screamed. Martin looked at the computer screen flashing. "Just another minute" he said, jumping out of the way of the sideways sliding VW™. "We have to keep a steady speed for 5 minutes."

There were disapproving noises coming from above, but the reindeer were too out of breath to complain. They continued their flight to nowhere, panting and gasping, tied to a sub-compact car. Sometime mid-flight, the Taco Teepee lunch hit the bottom of their digestive tract, forcing a long flatulent, whistling wind to blow.

"Oh Geez, Blitzen! Couldn't you have held that in?" Santa demanded.

"I told you not to get me a bean burrito!"

"Oh, that's nasty!" Martin plugged his nose and turned away, eyes tearing.

"Are we done yet?" Donner demanded.

"Yes," Martin said, hand still covering his face. He turned the knob on the ramp down slowing the sleigh to a crawl. The team of reindeer crash landed back onto the slightly moving tracks. They jogged to a stop with the final turn of the knob.

"That was easy." Smarty Marty smiled at Santa and the panting, heaving crew.

"Easy?" Vixen demanded.

"Fire the Air Traffic Controller!" Dasher yelled.

"Ok, enough!" Santa said. "Let's just finish and get out of here."

Ho, Ho, Hey! What Just Happened?

Marty looked at the computer screen, then turned to face Santa, his face ashen. "You failed," he said. "What?" Santa was furious. "How? Why?"

"Your vehicle has too high a concentration of noxious fume emissions."

The entire team turned and glared at Blitzen, who tried to shrink back into the crowd. Something difficult to do for a reindeer of his size.

"I told him not to eat it," Donner said.

"So what now?" Santa asked.

"Well, we can re-test your vehicle after we have corrected the problem," Marty answered. "But I'm not really sure how we can - - ummm - - -

"Plug him up?" Santa asked. "I do." He jumped off the sleigh and turned toward the door. "Where's the nearest drug store?"

"Across the street and down a block." Smarty Marty pointed.

Santa took off running, returning a few minutes later with a small bottle. Ripping the childproof, tamper proof, anal retentive 'you'll-never-get-into-me' seal, Santa spilled out a handful of small bean shaped pills into the palm of his hand. "Eat it!' he demanded, shoving his hand in front of Blitzen.

"What is it?" he asked. Santa held the bottle up so everyone could read it.

"Beano.™ Eat it!"

Blitzen chewed the pills and swallowed hard. "Fire that thing back up again, Marty," Santa yelled. "Problem has been fixed." He leaned over to Blitzen. "C-L-E-N-C-H" he growled into his ear. Santa grabbed the tailpipe probe, "or else," and jumped back into the driver's seat.

The knob turned.

The team launched.

The VW™ slid.

Ho, Ho, Hey! What Just Happened?

Numbers flew across the smogger's computer screen. When five minutes had passed, the knob again cranked off and the team crash landed in yet another heap on the ramp, this time swearing and spitting at Smarty Marty.

"Just wait till Christmas Eve this year you little runt," Dancer growled. "You're gonna get a real surprise, from us!"

Martin back away from the team, and faced his glued to the computer screen. "You passed!" he yelled, ripping the printout from the printer. "We did it!"

"Yes, we did, didn't we?" Santa said. "Thank you for your help, lad." Santa smiled. "I have the perfect gift for you this Christmas too." He took out his Blackberry and began typing into his notepad. 'Taco Teepee gift certificates, and a large bottle of Beano™ for Smarty Marty.' "Thank you, son. You've been very helpful."

"Yeah," Blitzen sneered through his bit, the other reindeer turning to glare Martin's direction. "You've been very helpful. We're going to have a special something for you this year."

"What does that mean?" Martin asked, scared.

"We can't tell you that now. It wouldn't be fair, would it?" Blitzen sneered again. "No one ever knows what their Christmas present will be, or Beano™, do they?"

Kringle vs. Kringle

Family Court; Case Number 11987642

"Here ye, here ye. Court is hereby called to order, the honorable Robert L. Rockingham presiding. All rise."

"Be seated," the judge ordered entering the room.

"All parties have been sworn in, your honor, in the matter of Dissolution of Marriage for Kristopher and Martha Kringle, Family Court Case Number 11987642."

"Thank you bailiff. Is counsel for both parties present?"

"Yes, your honor."

"Yes, we are your honor."

"Very well." The judge took off his glasses and looked out over his enormous oak bench at the parties seated before him. "Before we begin, let me make sure that I understand the situation correctly. We are here as a matter of discovery because the parties involved, one Kristopher and Martha Kringle, Aka: Santa and Mrs. Clause, cannot agree on the extent of the marital assets, let alone how to divide them. Am I correct?"

"Yes your honor." A nice looking young man in a tailored suit rose to address the court. Next to him was an elderly white haired woman. She was dressed in a red velvet floor length dress with a white fur lined collar

Ho, Ho, Hey! What Just Happened?

and sleeves. She wore thick soled, black knee-high snow boots. Her hair was circled in a bun at the back of her head, and she wore simple wire rimmed glasses. In her lap was a large ball of yarn and some plastic knitting needles, allowing her to get past courthouse security. She glared across the court room at her opponent, also dressed in red.

"It is our position that Mr. Kringle is hiding marital assets in order to deprive Mrs. Kringle of a fair settlement in these divorce proceedings."

"Liar!" the old woman blurted out, glaring at the table opposite hers.

"That's enough," the judge snapped. "You will control your client, counsel. Is that clear?"

"Yes, sir." He reached out and laid a reassuring hand on her shoulder. It had no effect. The glare continued.

"And," the judge continued, "I presume it is no accident that we are here today." He looked directly at Mrs. Kringle.

"I'm sure I don't know what you mean," she said.

"You don't know what I mean? It's December 24th. The busiest day of the year for your husband, and here we are in court on something that could have easily waited until after the holidays."

"We don't feel that way, your honor," her counsel chimed in. "The children depend on it."

"Yes, let's talk about the children for a second." The judge picked up a piece of paper and began to read. "In your complaint you state that you seek child support in the amount of $3 billion per month." He looked astonished at the complainant. "Am I reading this right?"

"She's not getting one dime from me!" Kris yelled out, drawing a sharp glare from the bench.

Ho, Ho, Hey! What Just Happened?

Another young man in a well tailored suit jumped to his feet and seated Mr. Kringle.

"If I may point out, your honor," her counsel said, "that's only $1 per child, per month. We feel this is a completely reasonable figure considering how many children there are in the world and Mrs. Kringle's responsibilities to each. Plus, we are only asking for support for those under the age of 10 as it is generally accepted that is the average age of belief."

"Average age of belief?" the judge asked. "What does that mean?"

"The age before doubt and cynicism sets in, sir."

"I see. So why not submit a formal child support request to the court for approval. Where is your Diss-o-master® showing income?"

"We don't have one. We can't prove income at this point in time."

"And why is that, counsel?"

"Because Mr. Kringle is claiming zero income."

"Zero?" The judge turned his attention to the other table. "How is that so, Mr. Kringle?"

"Simple, sir. I have no job."

"No job?" The judge was almost incredulous. "Then what do you call what you do every Christmas Eve, a hobby?"

"Yes, sir."

"And you expect me to believe that?" The irritation rising in the judge's voice was evident.

Mr. Kringle calmly rose to address the court. "Now Robert," he said to the judge, "you have three children. Have you ever once paid me anything for coming to your house and leaving toys for your little ones?" There was a stunned blank stare from the bench. "No," Santa continued, "and neither did your parents pay me for your presents when you were a little boy. Remember your first two wheeled bike? The red one?

Ho, Ho, Hey! What Just Happened?

Free. Completely free."

"Liar!" Mrs. Kringle blurted out again, this time pointing a crooked and frail finger out at him.

"Quiet!" Robert blurted out. He swallowed hard and shifted uncomfortably on the bench, turning back to address Mr. Kringle again. "Toys cost money. How do you acquire them?"

Santa smiled. "So, you've lost the magic of Christmas. It's okay, your honor. It happens a lot when young ones grow up. I have teams of elves that build things for me."

"And how do you fund this endeavor?" the judge inquired.

Santa's smile broadened. "Pure imagination."

"And so, it is your stance that since you have no actual income, it is not your responsibility to support these children monetarily in any way?"

"I am the one that makes and delivers those toys to them." Santa was angry now. His voice rising, face flush. "I am the one that risks my life out there in my sleigh in the worst weather of the year with young inexperienced reindeer trainees."

"Reindeer trainees?" the judge asked.

"You have no idea how hard it is to land on a slick roof and get those toys down the chimney without falling. And I have never once filed a work comp claim? No. Not once! Now I have that stupid DUI to fight on top of everything else. And what does she do? What part in this hobby does she hold? Nothing! She doesn't do anything!"

"Liar!" This time Martha Kringle rose. "I have been there by his side all these years, listening to all his endless stories and problems. I opened and sorted mail. I dictated responses. I maintained the naughty and nice lists and even upgraded it to his Blackberry™ so he could double check it en route on Christmas night. I cooked and cleaned up after all those filthy little elves, and for what? And now," her voice cracked, "after all these years- - -"

BANG!

Her rant was broken by the sound of a gavel being slammed down hard on the bench.

"Silence!" the judge screamed. He took a moment to compose himself, then turned to the parties before him. "As a matter of law, this point is simple. Since neither of you retains either physical nor legal custody of any of these children, there is no child support warranted. Actual income is irrelevant. Motion denied. Next issue."

Mrs. Kringle's attorney addressed the bench again. "Division of property, sir. We would like to have Mrs. Kringle retain the family residence in the North, and have Mr. Kringle move to the properties in the south."

"No!" Now it was Santa's turn to leap to his feet. "I can't run things from the South Pole."

"Why can't Mrs. Kringle move to the South Pole?" the judge asked.

"Your honor, we contend that it would be an enormous hardship on her to move so far away from her friends and her place of comfort."

"What friends?" Santa snapped. "The little elves she just called filthy?"

"Mrs. Kringle has built her entire life around Mr. Kringle and the North Pole. We feel that it is unfair to ask her to move since she is not the problem here."

"We feel," Santa's attorney chimed in, "that the hardship would be on Mr. Kringle if he were to move. There are no workshops set up down there, no supply sources. In addition, the weather is harsher, the commute more dangerous, not to mention more lengthy adding hours, if not days on to an already demanding schedule."

Ho, Ho, Hey! What Just Happened?

"Gifts are all delivered in a single night," Martha's counsel said. "A single night is still a single night no matter where you leave from."

"Your honor," Santa's attorney said, "everyone knows that the magic of Christmas is that gifts appear to be delivered in one night because Santa has the power to make time stand still, however in actual fact, it takes weeks, if not a month or longer to get all those presents out across the globe. In his aging years, this process has taken longer and longer. Mr. Kringle is not a young man. To stage these operations from another base would be costly and inefficient, especially on the busiest night of the year. We ask that he retain possession of the North property to continue with Christmas as usual and not run the risk of toys not being delivered in the confusion of it all."

Mrs. Kringle's attorney shot right back. "Your honor, he can make time stand still. Keep it still until the job is done right. There's no inconvenience here at all."

"He never made time stand still for me," Martha muttered under her breath.

The courtroom froze and turned to stare at her. She flushed.

The judge cleared his throat. He took off his glasses and looked kindly at Mrs. Kringle.

"Martha," he said softly, "what's really going on here?"

She looked down. "I don't know what you mean."

"Come on, now. We're here on Christmas Eve, the busiest and arguably most dangerous night of the year for the man you've been married to for how many years now?"

"Sixty-five."

"Sixty-five years. Wow! Frankly I don't even think I'll live that long, let alone be married that many years. You must love him a lot."

She nodded.

"But his work schedule is hard on you, isn't it?"

She nodded again.

He turned to the other table. "Santa, how soon after Christmas do you get started on the next year's toys?"

"The next day," Santa snapped.

The judge turned back to Martha. He shook his head in shame. "The very next day. And here you are, by his side, working, cooking, cleaning, organizing, and for what? You get no recognition at all, do you?"

Martha started to cry.

"When was the last time Kris took you on a vacation?"

"Our honeymoon," she whispered, "before he took this job".

"Sixty-five years ago?" The judge looked at Santa. "You should be ashamed of yourself... taking advantage of a beautiful, kind woman like this. She's done nothing but support you all this time and you have taken her for granted."

Santa's counsel was on his feet. "Objection, your honor. We contend that it is not easy being Santa. He has an extremely hard job."

"Sit down counsel. You can't object to me, and it's not a job, remember? It's a hobby."

He sat.

"Santa?"

"Yes, sir," he rose and addressed the judge.

"Does your power to make time stand still work all year long or just on Christmas?"

"It can work anytime during the year, but only once a year, and I need it for Christmas."

"Is there a time limit on it?"

"No, it will work for as long as I need it to.

Why?"

Robert leaned back in his chair. "It is the order of this court that as soon as Christmas is over, you are to continue to invoke your powers of timelessness and take your beautiful wife of sixty-five years on a vacation to show her how much you love and appreciate her. Furthermore, you are so ordered to continue this tradition every single year so long as you both live."

"But what if- - -"

BANG!

The gavel slammed again.

"So ordered." He looked out at his courtroom. "You, go deliver toys, and you pack for a trip. Merry Christmas to all."

Robert rose and exited the courtroom, black robes flowing behind him.

Santa stood and walked over to the table across from his. Smiling, he held out his hand. Martha slipped her tiny hand into his. "Why didn't you ever tell me?"

"I tried," she said, wiping a tear from her eye.

"I guess I don't listen very well. Where do you want to go?"

"Right now, home," she said.

"Home it is." He pulled her close, and with a twinkle of his eye, and a touch of his nose, the two disappeared from the courtroom leaving their respective counsels behind.

"Hey, did you get a billing address, by chance?"

Epilogue:

"So, apparently, nobody believes in elves." Martha stood at the front of the room addressing the group.

"Who said that?"

"The results are from a client survey that PR Consulting did," she said. "And, the nosey neighbors all think that you are foster children. They reported us to the Department of Education as aiding and abetting truant children, and now we have to home school all of you. As if I have time for that!"

"I don't want to go to school," the elves began to grumble.

"And I don't want to teach you all either, but if we don't then CPS is going to come in here and raid us all, so let's just get this over with. I thought we'd start with a history lesson. And, since it's relevant to what we all do, I thought we would go over the very first Christmas."

"Oh cool!" Ivan said. "I've always wondered about the first Santa."

"Actually," Martha said, "Christmas goes back way before the first Santa Clause. We go back over 2,000 years to the time of Caesar and Herod the Great."

"Harold? The Great what?"

"No, not Harold. Herod." Martha snorted.

"What kind of name is that?" The elves were all grumbling now.

Ho, Ho, Hey! What Just Happened?

"Who are they?" one elf apprentice asked.

"Sort of Kings, in old Roman times."

"Kings?" he said. "Roman kings? What do they have to do with Christmas? Did they even have Christmas then?"

"No, they didn't," Martha said. "But they have a hand in how it all started. Let me tell you how it began. You see, it all started with a legend."

"A legend?"

"Yeah, it's more than a story," she explained. "When a lot of people believe that something will happen it is a legend. Some called it faith, or a promise from God. It was a belief that a baby king would be born that would save these oppressed people from all of their troubles. They called him a Deliverer."

"Santa's a deliverer!" the girls shouted.

"Not like that," Martha continued. "Everyone at the time was waiting for him to be born. Apparently the angels all knew that this little king was going to be born too."

"What are angels?" another elf asked.

"They're God's helpers."

"Oh, kinda like us elves?"

"Sort of, but not really. They do what they're told. Anyway, God sent them to tell this young woman that she would be the new king's mother, and that her baby would save all of mankind."

"Did she believe them?"

"Yes, she did. The problem was that she was engaged to get married, so for her to turn up pregnant was a huge scandal. You see, the man she was to marry wasn't the baby's father. God was his father. The baby king had to be perfect, and we all know that humans are far from perfect!" She laughed.

"Ohhhh! Dirt!" The elves all giggled and nudged each other.

Ho, Ho, Hey! What Just Happened?

"Apparently the man wasn't so accepting either," Martha said. "So, the angels had to go pay him a visit too."

"Did they beat him up? Like the Sopranos?"

"No, they just explained the situation to him and he accepted it too. Apparently, angels can be very persuasive. So, they got married and had this little baby boy. He was born in a manger because they had to travel."

"A manger?" Ivan was perplexed.

"It's kind of a barn. It's an outdoor kinda thing."

"Wow! How exciting is that?" Ivan said sarcastically. "Another baby is born. Woo Hoo!"

"But, when he was born, all of the angels began singing," Martha said, "up in heaven."

"All of them?"

"All of them! Tens of thousands of them. Trumpets were blowing up in the sky. It was a huge party. There was a lot of noise. There were some good kings too," Martha told them. "Some people called them wise men."

"Like I said, the Sopranos!"

"Not the Sopranos! Wise men, not wise guys. Anyway, there were three of them. They traveled a long way to bring the new baby king some very expensive presents."

"Why would they do that?"

"Duh! Ivan," one of the younger elves said. "Everybody gets presents on their birthday. Try and keep up."

"Why such a big party? For a baby?" The younger elves were now looking to Ivan for the answers. He shrugged and looked back to Mrs. Clause.

"He's not just a baby, he's a baby king, and there's more to it than that. You see, the other king that I told you about, Herod. He was so afraid of this legend, he

Ho, Ho, Hey! What Just Happened?

sent soldiers out to find the little baby. The king found out somehow that it was true and that he really was going to be born. Herod was very scared."

"Why did he send soldiers?" Everyone was confused now, and listening intently to the story.

"Because he was not a very nice king, and the trouble that the baby king was going to save the people from - was him!"

"Oh!" The elves began to understand now. "Did the soldiers find him?" they asked.

"No, for two reasons. First the baby king's mother and father got wind of what was happening and they fled to another country with him to hide. I think the angels helped on that one. And second, the soldiers didn't really know who they were looking for. They just knew that it was a young boy under the age of two."

"So what did the soldiers do when they found all of the other little boys then?"

"Well, that's the sad part of the story. They killed them."

"They killed them! All of them?"

"Naughty List!" one elf started screaming. "Naughty List!"

"There was no naughty list back then," Martha said. "I told you, this was a very mean king who did not want anything to threaten his power or hold over these people. It was called the Slaughter of the Innocents."

"Poor little babies." The female elves were all crying now.

"And this is what we celebrate?" Ivan was disgusted.

"Not exactly. Even though there was a bad part in the beginning, the baby king survived. His parents and the angels kept him hidden and protected until he grew up."

"Go helpers!" The little elves were excited. "I

love angels."

"I don't think I'd want to meet one in a dark alley," Ivan mused.

"Anyway," Martha went on, "this king grew into a great man, who did save all of his people. He delivered them from their troubles, and taught them all how to live together in peace, and to love each other. He gave them hope. That's why the first Santa started doing what he did. He was celebrating this baby king's birth, and trying to be like him, the best way he knew how."

"So the first Santa was just trying to be like this king? He was a deliverer too!"

"Yes, but a different kind. Santa delivered presents, not people."

"And the first elves were just trying to be like the angels? Little helpers, right?"

"Yeah, I guess that would be true too."

"Wow, what a cool story. So, how did this man actually become the king?"

"That takes us into a different holiday, so that will have to be another lesson. I have a call in to the Easter Bunny to check the facts on that one."

"He has two holidays? Wow!" Ivan was smiling now. "He must have been a really great king."

"He was, and still is." Martha smiled. "His name is Jesus."

Ho, Ho, Hey! What Just Happened?

Ho, Ho, Hey! What Just Happened?

"Merry Christmas to all,
and to all a good night."
~Santa Clause

~'Twas the night before Christmas
Clement Clarke Moore

Loretta Sinclair
http://www.SinclairInkSpot.com

Blogs: (Both on my Sinclair Ink Spot website)
Jesus is my life coach
The impossibilities blog

Find me on: Facebook, Twitter, and LinkedIn

"For unto you, is born this day,
In the City of David,
A Savior…
And his name shall be Jesus.

~The Holy Bible, NIV (paraphrased)

Ho, Ho, Hey! What Just Happened?

Ho, Ho, Hey! What Just Happened?

Ho, Ho, Hey! What Just Happened?